WHOOPI GOLDBERG

Sugar Plum Ballerinas

in **Two Acts**

WHOOPI GOLDBERG

Sugar plum Ballerinas

in Two Acts

BOOK ONE

PLUM FANTASTIC

BOOK TWO

TOESHOE TROUBLE

WITH **DEBORAH UNDERWOOD**

ILLUSTRATED BY **MARYN ROOS**

DISNEP • JUMP AT THE SUN

LOS ANGELES   NEW YORK

Plum Fantastic text copyright © 2008 by Whoopi Goldberg
Plum Fantastic illustrations copyright © 2008 by Maryn Roos
Toeshoe Trouble text copyright © 2009 by Whoopi Goldberg
Toeshoe Trouble illustrations copyright © 2009 by Maryn Roos

All rights reserved. Published by Disney • Jump at the Sun, an imprint of Disney Book Group. No part of this book may be reproduced or transmitted in any form or by any means, electronic or mechanical, including photocopying, recording, or by any information storage and retrieval system, without written permission from the publisher. For information address Disney • Jump at the Sun, 125 West End Avenue, New York, New York 10023.

First Edition of *Plum Fantastic*, October 2008
First Edition of *Toeshoe Trouble*, May 2009
First Bind-Up Edition, May 2020
10 9 8 7 6 5 4 3 2 1
FAC 026988-20087
Printed in the United States of America
This book is set in 13 pt. Baskerville BT
Designed by Roberta Pressel and David Hastings

Library of Congress Control Number for Plum Fantastic: 2009278915
Library of Congress Control Number for Toeshoe Trouble: 2010502945
ISBN 978-1-368-05459-1
Visit www.DisneyBooks.com

SUSTAINABLE FORESTRY INITIATIVE

Certified Sourcing
www.sfiprogram.org
SFI-00993

Logo Applies to Text Stock Only

BOOK ONE
PLUM FANTASTIC

Chapter 1

I look at myself in my bedroom mirror—the mirror with little pink ballet shoes painted around it, which is on top of the dresser with the little pink ballet shoe drawer handles, which is beside the lamp with the little pink ballet shoes on the shade, which is next to my bed, which has—you guessed it—little pink ballet shoes on the comforter and pillowcases.

You might think the person who just moved into this room likes ballet. You would be wrong. My mom is the ballet-crazy one. Ever since I was born, she's had her mind set on one thing: turning me into a ballerina. She even stuck me with Petrakova for my middle name. Alexandrea *Petrakova* Johnson! The closest I've ever been to Russia is Atlanta. At least until we moved here to Harlem last week.

After I packed all my ballet stuff up, I told one of the Muscle Men Movers it would be okay if they lost that particular box. I even

wrote *lose this box* on the side in purple felt pen in case they forgot.

But when Aunt Jackie dropped us off at our apartment on 123rd Street, there it was, right on top of the mountain of moving boxes in our living room. So out came the ballet mirror and

the ballet lamp and the ballet comforter and the ballet pillowcases. They looked bad enough in my old room, but at least I'd gotten used to them there. My new room is a wall-to-wall ballet nightmare. The good thing is that we're way up above the street. Maybe if I put my fan just right, the ballet stuff will blow out the window.

Just as I think that, I look at the ballerina posters on the wall (all courtesy of Mama, naturally). There's Maria Tallchief, who danced with the New York City Ballet. Virginia Johnson, who was the prima ballerina of the Dance Theater of Harlem. Janet Collins, the first black prima ballerina of the Metropolitan Opera Ballet. They stare down from their frames with stern looks on their faces, their eyes fixed on me as if they can tell I'm thinking Bad Ballet Thoughts.

The only person on my wall who's smiling is my idol, champion speed skater Phoebe

Fitz. Aunt Jackie gave me an autographed poster of her for my last birthday. Phoebe looks as out of place among all the ballerinas as I feel in my ballet-themed room. I imagine Phoebe giving me an encouraging wink; then I turn back to the mirror.

A skinny nine-year-old looks back at me. I have Mama's brown skin and my dad's mixed-up eyes—one is green and one is brown—and my hair is dark and wavy, just long enough to stick in a ponytail.

Phoebe Fitz is really strong. She does one hundred push-ups every day. I can only do twenty-three so far, but I'm pretty sure I can see arm muscles popping out already.

I look good, except for one major problem: I'm wearing a big old pink puff pastry, the tutu to end all tutus. Layers and layers of netting droop down to my knees. Little rhinestones sewn into the netting glint like diamonds in pink marshmallow cream. A row of pink roses marches around my waist, and silver ribbons flutter when I move.

Ugh. I'll bet Phoebe Fitz never had to wear a tutu.

"Mama, you *know* we aren't supposed to wear this junk to class!" I yell down the hall. No response.

I march into her workroom, the tutu flopping up and down like it's trying to take off. There are moving boxes everywhere, but instead of unpacking, Mama's gluing huge feathers onto what was once probably a nice hat. She mostly makes costumes, but she's been on a hat kick lately. I know Mama is very talented—lots of people have said so—but to *me*, that hat looks like an ostrich's backside. Loose sequins in a rainbow of colors shimmer on the floor.

Mama doesn't notice me come in. Normal people hang out in jeans at home, but not her. She's wearing one of her creations; she calls it the Gold Mine Dress. She got the idea for it from a book about the California gold rush. The skirt of the dress is supposed to look like a mountain, so it flares out at the bottom. When Mama's standing still, the only colors you see are chocolate brown and gray, like soil and rocks, but when she moves you can see flashes of gold from the shiny threads and beads she's sewn deep into the creases. She loves it, but says it doesn't read well onstage. That means it looks good close up, but from far away you'd miss the interesting details. ("Interesting details" are things that make clothes special. I wish my tutu did not have so many of them.)

The hat she's working on would read well onstage even if the stage were on Mars and you were looking at it from Earth. "Fabulous . . . *mm-mmm*, perfect; maybe one more orange . . ." she says to herself as she chooses feathers and holds them up to the hat to see how they look.

The ballet school letter is lying by her sewing machine. I wave it in front of her face. "Mama!"

She looks up, a little dazed. I'd be dazed too if I'd been staring at purple and orange feathers all morning. "Why, Alexandrea!" she says, standing up to look me over. "You look wonderful. All ready for class?"

"Mama, listen to this." I read from the letter. *"Students at the Nutcracker School shall wear standard ballet leotards and tights. Dress code shall be strictly enforced."*

Mama puts down the feathers. "You *are* wearing a leotard. It's fabulous and *unique*. Can you imagine how it will stand out onstage?" She strikes a dramatic pose, as if an audience of 3,000 were watching her every move.

Sure, the tutu would look great onstage. However, I am not going onstage. I am going to a ballet class at a strange school in a strange city. Mama seems to have missed this critical point.

"And it doesn't say you can't wear a tutu over the leotard," Mama continues. "You *are* wearing those gorgeous tights I set out for you, yes?" She tries to peek at my behind, but I hold the tutu down. The tights I'm wearing are one of Mama's favorite creations. The legs look like normal tights, but the rear end is covered with shiny pink lightning bolts. You have to wear them over your leotard, not under, or you wouldn't be able to see the lightning (which would be fine with me). Mama calls the outfit Girl Power—Girl for the tutu and Power for the lightning. She says the contrast between the delicate tutu and the powerful lightning makes an interesting artistic statement. The dress code says we're supposed to wear tights, not interesting artistic statements. At least no one will see them under the tutu.

"Mama, *pleeeeease*." Thinking about the new ballet class makes my stomach hurt. I won't know anyone. I won't know where the bathroom is. And on top of all that, I get to walk in looking like an electrified bride on a wedding cake.

Mama drops the feathers and puts her hands on her hips. "Alexandrea, that is enough. When I was growing up, I dreamed of taking ballet from Ms. Debbé at the Nutcracker School, but my mother couldn't afford it. Now that my own little girl is going, she is going in style. Understand?"

It's hopeless. "Yes, ma'am."

"You only have one chance to make a first impression, you know," she says. "When they see you in that creation of mine, I guarantee you'll stick in their minds that way forever."

That's what I'm afraid of.

Chapter 2

Ten minutes later, we're walking down Madison Avenue. It's early June, and I'm hot and sticky in the jacket I threw on to hide my outfit. Horns honk and music blasts from cars and windows. Little kids run through sprinklers in the park across the street. Mama's happily pointing out places she knew when she was a kid. "That's where your Aunt Jackie and I played after school. . . . That's where my friend Roberta lived. . . ."

I'm not really listening. I'm thinking about Georgia. The street where we lived was quiet, with big trees and lots of grass. My best friend, Keisha, lived down the street. Best of all, the Apple Creek ice rink was just two blocks away. Last summer, Keisha and I went almost every afternoon.

One day Mama came to the rink to walk me home. "I've got a surprise," she said as we walked through the grass oval in the middle of Leland Park. "You and your mama are moving to Harlem." She had a big old grin on her face, like this was the best news in the world.

I stopped walking. I felt all shivery and clammy and prickly, like someone had tossed a bucket of Coke on me.

"Why?" I asked. But in my heart, I already knew. The bridal shop Mama owned always had a lot of customers. Mama showed them her fabulous designs: the Japanese-inspired kimono gown with fabric cherry blossoms trailing behind; the purple straight-up-and-down dress with the matching straight-up-and-down hat that looks like an oatmeal box; the fire-and-water dress that has flames of orange and red beads licking its hemline and a river blue shawl. But the brides all wanted normal white wedding dresses with normal white veils.

Mama sat on the ground. She took my hand and pulled me down beside her. The cool grass tickled the backs of my legs. "Honey, if I have to make one more boring wedding dress, I'll go crazy. I've always dreamed of having my own costume business, and you know it won't happen here in this little town. I want to do better—better for myself, and better for you."

I didn't need her to do any better for me. We had a nice house. We had a van. I had ice skates. I didn't need anything else. I started to tell her, but she kept talking.

"And I miss New York. I only moved here because of your daddy, and you know how long it's been since he passed."

My dad died when I was just two. It

sounds weird, but I don't really miss him, because I can't even remember him.

Mama said there was lots of potential in New York, because of all the theaters on Broadway. She said it would be great to live close to Aunt Jackie, who owns a hair salon and could braid my hair in all sorts of fancy ways.

I folded my arms across my chest. "Are there ice rinks there?" I asked.

"Yes, including a very famous one," she said. "And so many cultural opportunities. You'll love it. A change will be good for both of us." She stood and pulled me up. "Now what would you say to a triple scoop of Chocolate Coma ice cream? I think I hear it calling your name."

Before I knew it, Mama sold our van, because, she said, no one drives in New York. (If no one drives here, who's in all these cars?) And three weeks later we'd moved into a stuffy apartment on the third floor of a building called a brownstone. There's not even an elevator—just a creaky stairway that sounds as if it should be in a haunted house. (I run up the stairs really fast in case there are any ghosts around.)

So now I'm walking down a noisy Harlem street with a river of sweat pouring down my back. One thing about New York: Mama fits in a lot better here. Some people stare at the Gold Mine Dress. But they stare in an admiring way, not in the what-on-earth-is-she-wearing-now? way they did in Apple Creek.

Still, I'd rather be home. If I were, I'd be heading out right about now to skate with Keisha. "Where's the famous ice rink?" I ask.

"It's down at Rockefeller Center," Mama says. "We can go there when it gets cold." A fire engine zooms by, lights flashing and siren screeching. I plug my ears till it passes.

"Mama, how am I going to win an Olympic speed skating medal if I don't skate till it gets cold? Everyone knows you gotta practice all the time."

"Baby, speed skaters wear boring old body-suits—"

"Skin suits," I interrupt.

"Boring old skin suits, then. They are aesthetically unappealing. All those speed skaters look exactly the same. They look like the little guys in that old chocolate factory movie."

"Oompa-loompas?" I say. "Oompa-loompas are short and orange. Can you name one short orange speed skater?"

She goes on as if I hadn't said anything. "Ballerinas get to wear beautiful costumes."

"But, Mama . . ."

An old man pushing a shopping cart nearly runs over my foot. Mama yanks me out of the way.

"You need to pay attention, Alexandrea," she

says. "We aren't in Apple Creek anymore. Here in Harlem you need to use your city smarts." Just as she says this, a girl about my age races by on a skateboard, knocking into Mama's bag.

"Sorry!" the girl yells out as she passes. She screeches to a stop in front of a building, and her baseball cap flies off. She scoops it up, flips her board into the air, catches it, and races up the steps.

As the door slams behind her, I look at the glass sparkling over the doorway. THE NUT-CRACKER SCHOOL OF BALLET, the gold letters read. In smaller letters below, it says, WE TURN LITTLE GIRLS INTO LITTLE LADIES.

Mama hmmphs. "If the sign is right, they've got some work to do with *that* little girl," she says.

I glare at the sign above the door as Mama pulls me up the stairs. She can make me take ballet. She can make me wear a twinkling tutu. But *no one* is turning me into a little lady.

Chapter 3

Mama pushes open the door, and we go inside. The Nutcracker School is the weirdest-looking ballet school I've ever seen. Well, okay, I guess I've never actually seen a real ballet school before. My ballet class in Apple Creek was held in a church-Sunday-school building. All the classrooms were in a neat row off the main hallway. We met in the biggest room, where they had the church potlucks. The bathroom was at the end of the hall, with a big sign telling you where it was so you didn't have to ask anyone.

The Nutcracker School looks like a super-size house. There's a little office right at the front, and a room off to the left where girls are sitting and waiting for their class. Some of them look up as we pass. They're all dressed like the kids in my Apple Creek ballet class were: in normal ballet clothes. I was hoping that all the parents in New York ignored dress codes. Nope.

A sign saying CLASS IN SESSION hangs from a wooden door on the right. I wonder if there's just one classroom till I see the staircase leading up to the next floor. The sounds of piano music and thuds—maybe people practicing their jetés (that means "jumps," in ballet talk)—are coming from upstairs. Every time there's a thud, the chandelier above the stairs rattles, and the ceiling creaks as if it's going to break.

Also, I do not see any bathrooms. Maybe people in New York just hold it.

A tall, handsome man with caramel-colored skin and a short beard comes down the stairs, sees us, and smiles. He's wearing a bright white T-shirt and stretchy black pants, and he smells like pine trees.

He sticks out his hand. "I'm Mr. Lester. You must be Mrs. Johnson."

Mama takes his hand. "*Ms.* Johnson. I'm not married." She gives him a big, toothy smile. I roll my eyes.

"And you must be Alexandrea." He turns to me. "I'm one of the teachers here."

I try not to look surprised. We didn't have men ballet teachers in Apple Creek.

"Would you like to take off your coat?" he asks.

I shake my head. Mama gives me a look. I slowly peel off my jacket, hoping it's smashed some of the puff out of my tutu. But the skirt pops right back out, like one of those monsters in a scary movie that you think is dead until it jumps up and kills someone. Some of the girls in the waiting room stop talking to gape at me.

Mr. Lester's eyes fly open. "What an . . . uh, interesting outfit," he says.

"I made it myself." Mama beams. "It's one of a kind."

"It certainly is," Mr. Lester murmurs. "But Alexandrea might be more comfortable wearing a plain leotard next time."

Mama ignores this. "Alexandrea has been *so* looking forward to meeting Ms. Debbé," she says, which is a total lie. "It's her dream to be a prima ballerina with the Harlem Ballet, just like Ms. Debbé was." This is a total lie, too! I've never even heard of the Harlem Ballet. Next time she tells me not to fib, we are definitely having a discussion.

"I'm afraid Ms. Debbé is away at a dance teachers' conference," Mr. Lester says. "I'll be teaching Alexandrea's class today."

"Lucky Alexandrea," Mama says, winking at him.

I've had about all I can take of this. "Mama has to go now," I say in a loud, clear voice. "She has some very important costumes to make." I nudge her toward the door.

"Make me proud, sugar," Mama calls. She waves at Mr. Lester from the steps.

"Now, Alexandrea," Mr. Lester says. "Most of the nine-year-olds are in the Ballet Three class. We'll try you out there and see how you do. Any problems, you come talk to me. Okay?"

I nod. I wonder if I can keep up with kids who have been going to a big-city ballet school.

Mr. Lester takes me on a tour. We clomp up the stairs to the second floor, where there are studios. There's a big room on the third floor where they do their shows. There's a little room where they store costumes and music, and Ms. Debbé has an office down a hallway.

And there are bathrooms. Whew.

He takes me back downstairs to the room where the girls are waiting for class. "I'll leave you here," he says. "Class will start in ten minutes." He smiles at me. "I know it's not easy being the new kid, but I think you'll have a good time. It's a nice bunch of girls."

"Yes, sir," I say. I take a deep breath and go in.

Chapter 4

The waiting room gets quiet when I walk in. A few girls sitting near the door snicker. I hang my jacket on one of the hooks lining the wall, head to the bench farthest from the snickering girls, and start to sit down. Then I remember the lightning bolts on my behind. They make a weird crinkling sound when you sit on them. I stay standing.

I see the girl with the skateboard. I blink. She's sitting with two other girls. All three of them have skin so black it almost looks blue, and high cheekbones, like models are supposed to have. Their faces are almost identical. But the skateboard girl has muscles like she's on the Phoebe Fitz Push-Up Program, and the girl in the middle looks like she eats the skateboard girl's dessert for her. The one on the end is skinny but not muscley. She has her hair tied back with pink ribbons. The rounder one is holding a notebook and gazing off into space.

The wall in front of me has framed posters from the Harlem Ballet that Mama just mentioned—I guess it really does exist. I pick out one poster and focus on it. Maybe if I stand still, like a statue, everyone will forget I'm there.

But one girl marches right up to me. Her

honey-colored hair falls in spi-
ral curls around her shoulders, and she's wearing a
bright red-and-orange leo-
tard with green tights. Her
outfit stands out almost as much as mine does,
but she doesn't look one bit embarrassed.

"Girl, what *are* you wearing that crazy
thing for?" she asks in a loud voice.

I stare at her. In Georgia it's not nice to
point out weird stuff about people. A man
could walk down the street with a pig on his
head and everyone who saw him would just
smile and say how nice the weather was.

She gazes back at me with brown eyes, eyes
that look like they don't miss a thing. She
seems to be waiting for an answer.

"My mama made me," I explain.

"Wow. You got one *loca* mama," she says,
shaking her head.

"Loca?"

"I guess you don't know Spanish. *Loca* means 'crazy,'" the girl says. She starts warming up one foot at a time, drawing circles in the air with her toes.

My ears start to burn. Sure, *I* think Mama's a little crazy, but that doesn't mean some strange kid gets to say so.

"Did your mama pick *your* outfit?" I ask. "'Cause she might be *loca*, too."

Will this make the girl mad? I get my best don't-you-mess-with-me look ready, just in case. But instead she smiles and spins around like a fashion model. "You like it? I dyed the leotard myself. Actually, I dyed it because I spilled spaghetti sauce on it. My parents own an Italian restaurant, so lots of my clothes end up orange. I'm Epatha. Who are you?"

"Alexandrea," I say.

"You're from the South, right? My second-grade teacher was from Atlanta, and he talked like you."

All these people sound funny to me—I'd forgotten I must sound funny to them, too. I nod. "I just moved here."

"*Benvenuta.* That means 'welcome' in Italian," she says.

She sounds like she really means it. I smile.

"Are you Italian or Spanish?" I ask.

"I'm part Italian, part Puerto Rican, and all fabulous," she says, doing another twirl. I laugh, and she grins back at me.

"So you can speak Italian *and* Spanish?"

She shrugs. "My Puerto Rican grandma and my Italian grandma both live with us." She takes a purple ponytail holder off her wrist and twists her hair back into a bun. "I'm the only one in our family who speaks everything. My dad says I should come with subtitles."

I look over at the skateboard girl and the others again. "Are those girls triplets?"

"Yup," says Epatha. "JoAnn has the skate-board. Jerzey Mae is on the end, with the pink ribbons. Jessica writes poetry. One of her legs is shorter than the other, so she wears special shoes."

I'm trying to remember all this. I'm thinking so hard I almost forget how I'm dressed.

Two girls in pink leotards walk in. They both have their hair pulled back into buns. One of them is wearing a sparkly tiara. "I didn't know it was Halloween," Tiara Girl says to her friend as they walk past me. They dissolve in nasty giggles.

"Don't worry about them," Epatha says. "They think they're all that, and they ain't."

I'm impressed, both by her attitude and by the fact that she says "ain't." If I said "ain't," Mama would ground me for a week.

"Look at the way they walk," she continues. "Their feet stickin' out like duck feet. They saw a ballerina walk like that in a movie, I bet." She looks at them. "Quack," she says loudly. "Quack, quack."

Mr. Lester walks in and claps. "Time for class, ladies."

By now there are almost two dozen of us in the room. We follow Mr. Lester up the stairs to a studio on the second floor. A long barre runs along the window side of the room. The other wall is covered with mirrors. An old lady with bright red hair and green glasses is playing wild jazz on a piano.

"Class is starting now, Mrs. Buford," Mr. Lester tells her.

She sighs as if he's cramping her style. She stops playing.

Mr. Lester tells us all to sit on the floor. Epatha gives me a funny look. I hope she can't hear the lightning crinkle. I sit very still.

Mr. Lester welcomes us to the Nutcracker School's Ballet Three class. He tells us Ms. Debbé will teach the class most of the time, and that the class meets two times a week: Tuesdays and Saturdays.

"I'm pleased to announce that we have two new students with us. When I call your name, please stand up. . . ."

He looks at me. I shake my head wildly. In this getup, the last thing I need is more attention. He stops for a minute, then says, ". . . Or just raise your hand, so we know who you are."

I decide Mr. Lester is okay.

"Candace," Mr. Lester calls out. A mousy-looking kid pops up and down fast like a jack-in-the-box.

"Welcome, Candace. Alexandrea?" he says.

I raise my hand.

"Alexandrea just moved here from Georgia," he says. "We hope you'll enjoy our class."

"Yes, sir," I say.

"*Sir?*" says Tiara Girl. A few other girls laugh.

"In the South, children are taught to respect adults. Not a bad idea," Mr. Lester says. Tiara Girl snorts.

He continues. "I know you'll all be excited to hear about the show we'll be doing at the end of this session."

Epatha pokes me and whispers, "The best kid gets to be the Sugar Plum Fairy and do a dance all by herself."

Whoa. I thought the Sugar Plum Fairy was a Christmas thing. I wonder if New York is like Australia, where the seasons are all mixed up and Christmas comes when it's hot out.

"I'm gonna be the Sugar Plum Fairy this year," Epatha says. She turns to a short girl behind us. "Right, Terrel?" Her eyes glint, as if she knows she's asking for trouble.

The girl is padded with what looks like baby fat, but she's still small; she's definitely younger than any of the other girls here.

Terrel exhales heavily, as if they've been over this a million times before. "You are *not*. I am," she whispers. She's got long braids tied up in a bun, and the crookedest teeth I've ever seen. When she eats a sandwich, the bite marks must look like they were made with those zigzag scissors Mama uses for sewing. I run my tongue behind my own teeth and feel how smooth and even they are.

Mr. Lester continues. "But I'll let Ms. Debbé tell you more about that when she returns next week. Now, ladies—barre, please. First position."

Everyone stands up and takes a place at the barre. We put our feet in first position, which is when your heels are together and your toes stick out. The piano lady starts playing tinkly ballet music.

"Demi-plié . . . grand plié . . . demi-plié . . . and up," Mr. Lester says as we bend our knees and go down to the floor, then back up, just like in my old ballet class. Epatha's in front of me, making arm gestures bigger than everyone else's. Every once in a while she adds in her own little jumps or arm swirls, but Mr. Lester doesn't seem to mind. When we turn around to do the other side, I'm behind Terrel. Her movements are tight and precise, as if she were in the ballet division of the U.S. Marines.

I can already tell this will be harder than my old class. My teacher in Apple Creek, Miss Gutchings, was about a hundred years old. She wore thick glasses that made her eyes look huge, but she still couldn't see us very well. She'd show us a move, then sit down in her chair and try to stay awake while we practiced it by ourselves.

Mr. Lester is definitely no Miss Gutchings. He's coming around and correcting each of us, moving an arm here, a leg there. Nothing gets by him. I haven't seen some of the barre exercises before, so I try to copy whoever's in front of me. Mr. Lester can always tell when I'm faking it. He comes by and quietly shows me the right way to do each new move.

After our barre work is done, Mr. Lester asks us to gather in the center of the room. We make a big circle.

"Let's do some turns," he says.

Uh-oh. Turns are not my strongest move. When you do turns, you're supposed to spot. That means you look in one place, then turn your head fast and look at the same place again. It keeps you from getting dizzy. But I just can't do it.

Keisha says I am spotting-impaired. When my class did turns in Apple Creek, I always crashed into the wall, unless I crashed into another girl first. Once I crashed into the watercooler and flooded the studio, which got even Miss Gutchings's attention. After that she made me sit on the side of the room during turns practice.

But that was a whole month ago. I've probably gotten better since then.

"We'll do simple chaîné turns." Mr. Lester

stands in front of us and does a series of turns, moving in a perfectly straight line along the mirrors. "We'll travel clockwise around the room."

The piano lady plays. Everyone starts doing neat turns. Everyone, that is, except me.

After just two turns, the room is whirling, and I can hardly stand up. I crash into the girl with the braids. "Sorry," I say.

I crash into Tiara Girl. "What is wrong with you?" she says.

I crash into the end of the barre. My tutu gets stuck on it. I hear a ripping sound, but luckily I don't see any holes when I inspect it.

Mr. Lester claps. "That's enough turning for today," he says loudly. I feel everybody's eyes on me. I look up at the ceiling.

"Let's practice our grand jetés," Mr. Lester says, eyeing me nervously.

Yes! That's one thing I'm good at. I love leaps. I saw a TV show about animals called gazelles that live in Africa. They look like deer, and they jump through the grass like nobody's business. When I do grand jetés, I feel just like a beautiful gazelle.

We form two lines, and two at a time we bound across the room. Epatha and I are second. We get a running start, then leap from one leg to the other.

"Very nice, Alexandrea," Mr. Lester calls as we walk back to the ends of our lines. Epatha bumps her shoulder against mine and grins. I beam.

A lady pops her head into the room. Mr. Lester goes over, and she says something to him.

"Keep going, girls," he says. "I'll be right back."

Epatha and I inch closer to the heads of our lines. Finally it's our turn again. I jump even higher this time, higher than Epatha. I soar through the air. I feel light, lighter than a balloon. The other girls gasp. I smile. I must be really good.

In midleap, I realize something is missing. My tutu. It's lying in a pile in the middle of the floor. And my pink-shiny-lightning-bolt-covered rear end is right out there, shimmering for everyone to see. I turn around to hide it, but it's

38

too late. Everyone's laughing. Tiara Girl's laughing extra loud.

The piano lady stops playing. She leans over the piano to get a good look and moves her glasses up and down as if she can't believe what she's seeing.

I run over and grab the tutu. The girls circle around me, still laughing their heads off. It's just like on the gazelle TV show, when one of the leaping gazelles gets surrounded by a pack of nasty lions ready to rip her to bits.

Epatha pushes through, carrying a sweatshirt. "What are you all looking at?" She ties the sweatshirt around my waist and marches me out of the center of the circle. "Y'all better start jumping again before Mr. Lester gets back," she calls over her shoulder. "Mrs. Buford—how about some music?"

The piano lady's painted-on eyebrows creep up to the top of her forehead, but she begins to play. The other kids get back into their lines and start leaping.

"Thanks," I say to Epatha. I crumple up the stupid tutu and cram it under a chair.

"De nada," she replies. "Don't worry about it."

Mr. Lester comes back. He sees the sweat-shirt around my waist but doesn't ask any questions. He's definitely okay.

After class, we all go downstairs to wait for our parents. I put on my coat fast and stuff the tutu into my bag. I'll tell Mama about the fashion disaster later.

Tiara Girl leaves with a tall woman in fancy clothes. "Bye, Electric Butt," she says with a smirk as she passes me.

I stick out my tongue at her back. Epatha grins.

Mama comes in and gives me a hug. "How'd it go, baby?"

I try to decide. "Okay, I guess."

"Did you make any new friends?" she asks as we walk down the steps.

Epatha and an older girl pass by us. "*A presto*—see you soon!" she calls to me as they turn down the street.

"Yeah," I say to Mama. "I think I did."

Chapter 5

The day after my first ballet class, I wake up when I hear Mama rattling around in her workroom. Not that it takes much to wake me up nowadays. It's hard to sleep in Harlem. The sounds of cars and music and talking drift up from the street to my bedroom window. I miss my room in Apple Creek. I miss the tree outside my window. I miss the squirrels that scampered around and tried to swipe each other's acorns.

"Morning, honey," Mama calls as I drag myself into the kitchen. She's wearing Queen of the Nile, a sand-colored pantsuit with a cascade of shimmering green and blue beads at the top. They narrow into a thin band that winds down the front and wraps around the left leg. The pantsuit is Africa, and the beads are the Nile River. I helped her find a map that showed exactly where the river twists and turns, so she'd know where to put the beads. The outfit is actually kind of cool, and she looks beautiful, as always. But sometimes I wish she'd just wear a robe at breakfast.

"What do you want?" she asks.

"Can I have oatmeal?"

"Oatmeal?" She stares at me like I'm nuts. "You've never had oatmeal in your life."

"I read in *Speed Skating Weekly* that Phoebe Fitz eats oatmeal for breakfast every single day," I say.

Mama rolls her eyes. "Even Phoebe Fitz wouldn't be crazy enough to stand over a hot stove cooking oatmeal when it's eighty-three degrees outside. Try again."

I sigh. "Okay. Cornflakes, I guess."

Mama goes to the cupboard and pulls out

a cereal box. It looks weird.

"Those aren't the right ones," I say. "There's supposed to be a scarecrow on the box."

"Honey, that's a Southern brand. They don't have it in New York. These are just as good." She pours milk over a bowl of cereal and sets it in front of me.

I shove my spoon into the bowl and stir the cereal around. "They're smaller. And lumpier. And they're a darker yellow."

"Alexandrea . . ."

"I'm eating them, I'm eating them," I say. If this place is so great, why can't they make normal cornflakes?

After I eat my unsatisfactory New York cereal, I help Mama unpack her workroom. She arranges bolts of fabric while I dump red, green, purple, silver, and gold sequins into little organizer drawers. I hang scissors from hooks on the wall. I put all the jumbled-up spools of thread in order, light yellow to dark yellow, light green to dark green, light blue to dark blue. We set hat stands around the room for all the fancy hats she's working on.

Pretty soon it looks just like her workroom back home. She steps back to admire our work. "A real, live, professional New York City costume studio," she said. "Now I can get to work advertising. With a little luck, those orders will start flying in."

They'd better. I heard her talking to Aunt Jackie last night. She said that moving here used up a lot of our money. No one's bought Mama's bridal shop back home yet. And even I know it costs more to live in a big city than in Apple Creek.

"I guess we'll have to move back if they don't," I say. I try to look disappointed at the prospect, but I can't keep the corners of my mouth from turning up. If we moved back, I could have the rest of the summer to skate with Keisha. And I could take ballet at a place where no one's crazy enough to make me do turns.

"Baby, this *is* our home now."

I try another tack. "If we can't afford my ballet classes, I understand."

She gives me a look. "Nice try. Now help me put these moving boxes away."

I sigh. Looks like I'm stuck—stuck in Harlem and stuck in ballet.

Chapter 6

Epatha is already at the Nutcracker School when I get there on Tuesday afternoon. She looks me up and down approvingly. "Much better."

I convinced Mama to let me dress like a normal person this time. I have on a light brown leotard and tights. Not only are they boring and non-attention-getting, but they may help me blend in with the floor if I keel over doing turns.

Epatha, however, would only blend in if she were in the middle of the Amazon rain forest. Her leotard and tights have all different kinds of green in them.

"No spaghetti sauce?" I ask.

She shakes her head. "I spilled pesto on these. You know what pesto is? It's green, 'cause it's made of ground-up *foglie*—leaves. You eat it on noodles."

Ground-up leaves? In Georgia people don't eat ground-up leaves. *Worms* eat ground-up leaves.

Two girls walk over to us. The taller one has dreadlocks and big brown eyes. The other one is Terrel, the short girl with crooked teeth who stood next to me in the last class. Today her braids are hanging down, and there's a butterfly barrette at the bottom of each one. She thrusts a stack of flash cards into Epatha's hand.

"*You* quiz Brenda," she says. "I can't even read some of these words. We don't learn about clavicorns in second grade."

"*Clavicles*," says Brenda. She takes the top

flash card from the stack Epatha is holding and waves it under Terrel's nose.

"Why can't doctors just say 'collarbone,' like normal people?" Terrel asks as she pulls her braids back into a bun.

Brenda points to a word on the card. "Okay, *collarbone*."

"Whatever," says Terrel.

"Hey, Brenda. Where were you on Saturday?" Epatha asks.

Brenda seems to give up on getting any flash card help. She takes the cards back and sits on the floor, plopping her books down next to her. "Mom my with museum science the at show planetarium a to went I."

"Y'all, this is Alexandrea," Epatha says. "She's from the South, and sometimes her mama makes her wear crazy tutus. And this is Terrel," she says, pointing to the short girl. "She's only eight, but she's really good at ballet, so she's in our class. This is Brenda. She's

49

going to be a doctor, so she studies all the time and talks backward."

I don't know if it's polite, but I have to ask. "Uh . . . why do you talk backward?"

"Backward wrote Vinci da Leonardo," Brenda says as she takes off her sneakers, which look old enough to disintegrate at any minute. "Smart really was he. Smarter get I'll, backward. . . ."

Terrel sighs loudly and holds up her hand to stop her. "Brenda, how's she supposed to understand you? She hasn't had a year to figure out backward talk like we have." She turns to me. "Some guy named Leonardo da Vinci wrote backward. He was real smart. So Brenda thinks if she talks backward, she'll get smarter. Like, it'll rewire her brain or something."

Brenda nods.

Terrel says, "Leonardo wrote each word backward, too, so *cat* turns into *tac*. Brenda tried talking like that, but even we couldn't understand her. So now she just puts the words in reverse order. It get?"

It get. I think for a second. *Get it.* I nod.

"We're the only ones who know what she's saying. It's useful when you're talking around grown-ups—it's like a code," Epatha adds.

"Me understand can't mom my even," Brenda says with a satisfied smile.

I'm trying to figure this out when Tiara Girl waltzes in with her friend. "How adorable," she says. "Gobbledygook Girl and Twisted Teeth are friends with Electric Butt." They sit down and put on their ballet slippers, leaving their sneakers under a bench.

Brenda ignores the girls—she's studying her flash cards again—but Terrel stares at them. When they disappear into the bathroom, she marches over and expertly ties Tiara Girl's shoelaces to the bench.

Just as Terrel returns, an older woman

glides into the waiting room. She's tall, and the green turban she's wearing makes her look even taller. Frosty green eye shadow pops out against her deep brown skin. She looks elegant and powerful all at the same time, like she's the queen of New York. She has a walking stick in one hand and a beautiful carved wooden box in the other.

She raises the stick into the air. Silence falls over the room.

"The class, it begins," she says. She turns sharply and heads upstairs, the filmy sleeves of her blouse trailing behind her. The stick thumps on each stair as she goes up.

"That's Ms. Debbé," Epatha tells me as we follow her up the stairs. "I bet she gives us the shoe talk."

"The what?" I ask.

"You'll see."

We sit on the studio floor. Ms. Debbé stands motionless in front of us. When the last girl sits down, Ms. Debbé sweeps her arm out to the side.

"Welcome to my ballet school," she says. Her accent sounds like that cartoon skunk's, so she must be French. "Here you will learn to move. You will learn to dance. But also, you will learn to live. Movement is dance. Movement is life. Dance is life." She looks around the room at us, as if she's daring us to say she's wrong.

What the heck is she talking about?

Epatha watches her raptly. Terrel looks at me and raises her eyebrows. Brenda's lost in space, probably thinking about clavicles.

Ms. Debbé opens the hinged lid of the carved wooden box. She takes out a pair of worn toe shoes and holds them in her hands so we can see them. "These shoes, these humble shoes"—she pauses dramatically—"are my most prized possession. They are the toe shoes of Miss Camilla Freeman." She shows us

53

the sole of the right shoe, which has a faded autograph written in black pen.

"Miss Camilla Freeman was my teacher when I first came to this country." She seems to stand even taller when she says this. "When Miss Camilla Freeman began dancing, people told her she would never be a star because of her color. But did she listen?"

She looks right at me and waits.

"Uh . . . no?" I say.

"No! She did not listen to those people, those foolish people. She worked hard. She became the first black prima ballerina in the Ballet Company of New York. Where she wore *these*." She waves the toe shoes in the air.

"These toe shoes," she continues, "represent potential. These toe shoes, they prove anything is possible."

"I'll bet those toe shoes prove shoes can still stink after fifty years," Epatha whispers to me. Ms. Debbé swivels her head to stare at

Epatha. Epatha shuts up fast.

"If you get discouraged, if you want to quit, if the amazing art that is the ballet seems too difficult for you, think. Think of these toe shoes." She tucks the shoes gently back into their box.

"Now. We talk about our show, our lovely show at the end of the summer."

You can tell most of the girls have heard the shoe talk before. Now they perk up and pay attention.

"This year, things, they will be different." Ms. Debbé raises an eyebrow and looks around the room, nodding her head.

Whispers fill the room. "Whoa. Things ain't never different around here," whispers Epatha. "The Ballet Three show is always the same. I know, 'cause both my sisters took this class."

"We will have some *thrilling* new dances," Ms. Debbé says.

Tiara Girl raises her hand. "Will we still have the Sugar Plum Fairy dance?"

"Oui, oui," Ms. Debbé says. "But that, too, will be different. Before, always we chose the best dancer in the class to be the Sugar Plum Fairy."

"Well, duh," Epatha whispers. "Who else would they choose—the worst dancer?"

Ms. Debbé continues. "Last week, I was at a meeting of dance teachers. At the meeting, we discussed potential. You all have the potential to be great dancers. So, this year, how will we choose parts? By pulling your names out of a hat. You will all have an equal chance to be the Sugar Plum Fairy."

Whispers fill the room. The grin slides off Epatha's face. Terrel looks determined. Even Brenda's brow is creased. "Applications college my on good look would part the getting," she whispers.

Terrel exhales heavily. "You're only nine,

girl!" she says. "You got seven more years to worry about college applications."

Ms. Debbé raps her stick on the floor for attention. "We draw the names next class. Once they're chosen, no changes. No arguing. You must bloom where you are planted, children. *Bloooom,* like lovely little flowers! Now. To the barre."

After class, everyone is still talking about the drawing. The good dancers are upset because they were expecting to be the Sugar Plum Fairy. The not-so-good dancers are excited, because they have a chance now. Then there's me—all I want is to make it through class without breaking any bones.

We pack up our things. There's a shriek from the other side of the waiting room.

"Who tied my shoes to the bench?" Tiara Girl cries.

Terrel grins.

I skip outside to meet Mama. Ms. Debbé

may think we all have potential, but I *know* I don't. As far as ballet goes, I am a potential-free zone. I don't care who gets the Sugar Plum Fairy dance, as long as it's not me. The good thing is, it's not going to be. There are twenty-three girls in the class, and I never win anything. I don't even win when *everyone* wins. At Keisha's birthday party, they drew names out of a hat for prizes. Every person was supposed to get a prize, but my name fell out of the hat. They found it two days later in a pile of crumbs under the refrigerator.

I may have to take ballet, but one thing's for sure: I'm safe from the Curse of the Sugar Plum Fairy.

Chapter 7

"Come on, Alexandrea—get that lovely outfit on so we can go," Mama calls.

I look around my room. I do not see any lovely outfit. I do, however, see a blue-striped sailor suit with a pleated skirt and a straw hat. It looks like something a kid would have worn over a hundred years ago. That's because it *is* something a kid would have worn over a hundred years ago.

Today Mama says we are going to "implement the marketing plan." This means she's made appointments at a bunch of theaters to introduce herself and her work. Unfortunately, she wants to show them that she can do historical costumes as well as modern ones. And she wants to show them what her work looks like on a real person. Which means I get to dress like a kid who's escaped from an 1880s orphanage.

Mama pops her head into my room. She's wearing her Iceberg Suit. She got inspired to make it after we watched *Titanic*. It's white with shades of shimmery blue like a glacier. There's a pointy triangular cap over each shoulder, and there's a pointy triangular hat that goes with it. She says dressing like an iceberg is good on days like today, because an iceberg is a force of nature that can bring down even the strongest ship. I guess that means everyone will have to hire her.

"Come on, honey," she says. "Can't you figure out how it goes on?"

"I can't figure out *why* it goes on," I mutter. But I pull on the skirt and the top. Phoebe Fitz gives me a sympathetic look from the poster on the wall.

"Adorable!" Mama says, spinning me around.

"If you get a lot of business today, we never have to do this again, right?" I say.

"Right," she agrees.

Ten minutes later, we're tromping down the street. Ladies are pointing at me, and I can hear them telling each other how cute I look.

"Isn't this fun?" Mama asks, adjusting her enormous white sunglasses. We each have a load of fancy brochures for her costume business in our arms. It's so hot I can already feel the bottom one getting slippery and wrinkled from my sweat.

Mama's set up appointments all over town. When we get to a theater, she sashays in like she owns the place. She plunks a brochure down and tells whomever's listening exactly why they need to hire her. Everyone is polite, and they all promise to keep her information on file.

"Isn't anyone going to hire you *today*?" I ask.

"That's not the way it works, Alexandrea," she says. "You need to plant some seeds and hope some of them sprout."

I would not be a good businesswoman, because I don't like waiting for seeds to sprout. When I planted flower seeds back home, I kept digging them back up to see if they were doing anything.

After hours of this, we head back up Broadway toward home. I spot a big building with a fancy marquee out front. They probably have lots of money to hire costume people. "There's another theater," I say. "Aren't we going in that one?"

We stop right in front. "The Harlem Ballet," Mama says. "That's where Ms. Debbé danced when she was young. I always wanted to go see her, but back then we couldn't afford it."

Mama gazes up at the building as if it's

some kind of church or something. I've never seen her like this before. She looks like she's scared to go inside.

Suddenly I forgive her for making me wear a goofy outfit and dragging me around in the sweltering heat. I take her hand and pull her toward the entrance. "Well, now you're here. What are you waiting for?"

We push open the heavy door together and walk up to the box office. "Can I help you?" the ticket lady asks.

Mama just stands there. I poke her. She clears her throat, then launches into her spiel. She pushes a flyer through the window so the ticket lady can see it, and asks if she can make an appointment to talk with a costume person.

Footsteps echo on the floor behind us. I smell pine trees.

"Alexandrea?"

Oh, great—It's Mr. Lester. You'd think in a big city you wouldn't run into people you know. Wrong. This is as bad as back home, where if you weren't careful you'd see your teacher holding hands with her boyfriend at the ball game or buying athlete's foot cream at the store.

"Hi," I say. He gives me a funny look. I'd almost forgotten my sailor suit. The man is going to think I don't have any normal clothes at all. He, on the other hand, looks good, with his dark jeans and crisp yellow shirt.

Mama turns around and smiles real big. "Hello, handsome," she says. Looks like she's back to normal—too bad.

He asks what we're doing there, and Mama shows him a brochure. Then she asks what *he's* doing there, and he says he's directing one of the dances in the Harlem Ballet's next show.

Wow—that sounds like a pretty big deal. I wonder what a hotshot director is doing teaching ballet to a bunch of kids. And I wonder if

I'm going to be even more of a mess in his classes now, because I'll be all nervous.

"Would you like to see the theater?" he asks.

What I'd really like is to get out of there before Mama says anything else embarrassing. But I've never seen the inside of a New York theater before.

"We'd love to," Mama says.

He takes us through the hall with its red velvet seats, past the heavy curtain, and backstage. He shows us the dressing rooms (which are small and not all glamorous—there aren't even stars on the doors). We see the room in the very back of the theater where they control the lights, and the place where they store the costumes. Mama sneaks some brochures onto the costume designer's desk when Mr. Lester isn't looking.

We walk onto the stage and look out at the house, the place where the audience sits.

There must be hundreds of seats. Even though they're all empty, my stomach jumps a little.

"To think Ms. Debbé danced on this very stage," Mama says, turning around slowly.

"Oh, yes. Mom still feels like this is her home," Mr. Lester says. "That's why the Nutcracker School has such close ties to this theater. Many of our students go on to dance here."

Mama looks confused.

"Ms. Debbé's your mom?" I ask.

"Yes. She kept her maiden name, since she was already well known when she got married," he says.

Mama starts to get all flustered again. I guess if I met Phoebe Fitz's kid, I'd be freaked out, too. Mama looks a little sick, as if she went on a roller coaster too many times.

Mr. Lester thinks the heat must be getting to Mama. He takes us to a coffee shop across the street and buys us some cold drinks, which is nice of him. We sit in the window. Mama recovers enough to ask Mr. Lester if he has any ideas about where she should take her brochures, and he writes down the names of a few of his theater friends for her.

As they chat, I look up and see a face right outside the coffee shop window. I can't believe it—it's Terrel. I flush as I see her wide-open

eyes go from Mr. Lester to Mama and back again. Okay, this is totally *worse* than Apple Creek. I wave halfheartedly to her as a guy who must be her brother grabs her arm and pulls her away.

We say good-bye to Mr. Lester and begin to walk home. "That man is certainly handsome. When I first met him I wondered . . ." Her voice trails off, and then she shakes her head. "Well, now that I know he's Ms. Debbé's son I could never go out with him. Imagine having Ms. Debbé as a mother-in-law! I'd be too scared to even talk."

I'm relieved by this. But I wish Terrel were around to hear it.

Chapter 8

It's Saturday before ballet, and rain is pounding against the studio windows. I'm sitting with Epatha and Brenda. Terrel hasn't shown up yet. I don't want her to be sick, but I wouldn't mind if she went on vacation for a few months. But no sooner do I think this than she appears and comes straight over to us.

"What were you doing in that goofy sailor suit, and is your mom dating Mr. Lester?" she asks me.

"Mr. Lester?" say Epatha and Brenda at the same time. At least they ignore the sailor suit part.

"Of course not," I say. "We just ran into him when we went to the ballet theater. And he took us out for drinks."

"To a *bar*?" Epatha shrieks.

"Are you crazy?" I ask her. "To a coffee shop. It was no big deal."

Terrel squints. "It looked like a date to me," she says.

My face gets hot. "Well, it wasn't. He thought my mom was going to pass out from the heat, so he bought her a soda. That's it." I can hear how defensive I sound, which is stupid, since I'm not lying. "Did you know Ms. Debbé is his mom?" I add, hoping to distract them.

It seems to work. "That knew everyone thought I," says Brenda.

"That crazy lady," Epatha says. "Why would she want to pull the Sugar Plum Fairy's name out of a hat? It needs to be someone really good, *una persona muy buena*. Someone like me, for instance."

Terrel raises her eyebrows.

"Or you," Epatha adds, to be fair. "Or Brenda." She glances at the book Brenda's face is buried in. "Gross! What the heck is that?"

Brenda looks up from a colorful drawing that shows all the blood vessels in the human body.

"Dead be we'd, them without and, vessels blood it's. Gross not it's."

Terrel translates for me.

"Well, it's making me *enferma*," says Epatha.

"That's 'sick' in Spanish," Terrel explains. "She says it all the time."

With all the translating she's doing, Terrel could work for the United Nations.

Tiara Girl comes over. "Just so you know, I'm going to be the Sugar Plum Fairy, so don't hold your breath."

"How do you know?" Terrel demands.

Tiara Girl smiles. "My dad gives this school a lot of money. He called Ms. Debbé last night and told her he wants me to be the star. Too bad *you* all don't have rich dads." She looks at us, especially at Brenda.

"Tiara that under around rattling brain a have don't you bad too," Brenda responds. As Tiara Girl is trying to figure out what she said, Mr. Lester comes in and claps.

"Class, girls," he says. He leads us upstairs, a long cardboard tube under his arm. He opens the studio door and we file inside.

Ms. Debbé drifts through the door carrying a top hat. It looks as old as Ms. Camilla Freeman's toe shoes.

"Ladies," she says. "It is our big day, the beginning of the exciting preparations for our performance. Your names, they are all in this hat. I will draw them. No funny business. No favorites." She gives Tiara Girl a tight smile.

Tiara Girl looks a little *enferma*.

Ms. Debbé continues. "First, we will have the Raindrop Ballet. The dancers will wear these lovely costumes." She nods at Mr.

Lester. He pulls a large paper out of the cardboard tube and unrolls it. It's a drawing of a blue leotard and blue skirt with little shiny raindrops hanging around the bottom. Most of the girls ooh and aah.

Brenda raises her hand. "Light refracts it way the of because blue looks just water."

Ms. Debbé looks at Terrel, who says, "She says raindrops aren't really blue."

Ms. Debbé replies, "Thank you, Brenda and Terrel. However, *our* raindrops *will* be blue. Now, then." She holds the hat. Mr. Lester pulls out six pieces of paper and reads six names. Six girls on the other side of the room high-five each other.

"Yes!" Epatha whispers when her name's not called. "I'm supposed to be a fabulous fairy, not a drippy raindrop."

"Next we have the Dance of the Animals," Ms. Debbé says. Mr. Lester holds up a paper showing ten different animal costumes.

Ms. Debbé reads off each animal, and then Mr. Lester pulls out a name.

Tiara Girl is a warthog. Epatha and Terrel laugh their heads off. Even Brenda smiles.

"Now, an exciting new dance I have just choreographed. It is called the Monster Ballet, and it will be very, very charming," Ms. Debbé says.

Mr. Lester unrolls the next paper. The costume looks like a big, hairy, purple grape. Everyone gasps. It is not a good gasp. This costume makes Tiara Girl's warthog outfit look like Cinderella's ball gown.

Brenda gazes at the picture with interest. "Bacteria coli E. like looks it," she says.

"What's E. coli bacteria?" asks Epatha.

"A germ that makes you throw up," Terrel says.

"*Sí*. Just looking at that picture makes me want to throw up," says Epatha.

"Our six little monsters will be . . . Brenda,

Terrel, Epatha, JoAnn, Jerzey Mae, and Jessica," Ms. Debbé says. Epatha sticks her tongue out the side of her mouth and collapses on the floor like she's been hit with an arrow.

I look around to see how the triplets are taking it. JoAnn looks bored. Jessica looks as if she's trying to make the best of it. Jerzey Mae looks like she's about to cry.

"Now, finally," Ms. Debbé says, "for our Sugar Plum Fairy."

Mr. Lester reaches into the hat.

Finally? I do some fast math in my head as she pulls the name from the hat. Six raindrops, ten animals, six monsters, twenty-three kids in the class . . .

Oh, no.

"Alexandrea will be our Sugar Plum Fairy this year," Ms. Debbé says, beaming at me. Mr. Lester holds up a picture of a white dress with a white, sparkling tutu. Naturally. Another tutu.

"You will love the dance, Alexandrea," Ms. Debbé says. "It is very fun. Lots and lots of turns."

I feel sick.

After class, Epatha and the other girls are less friendly to me. "Lucky you," Epatha says.

"Lucky, yeah," says Brenda, as she jerks her T-shirt over her head.

Terrel looks as if she'd like to tie my legs to a bench.

What is wrong with these people? Is it my fault my name popped out of that hat? I'd rather have to wear an 1880s sailor suit for the rest of my life than be the Sugar Plum Fairy. "I really wish it wasn't me," I say, trying to sound calm, the way Mama does when she's mad.

"Oh, sure you do," says Epatha. "It's *such* a burden to be a star."

"Are you *sure* your mom isn't going out with Mr. Lester?" Terrel asks.

My scalp begins to prickle. Getting the part was bad enough, but now they think I'm a liar on top of it?

"My mom is *not* going out with Mr. Lester, and I do *not* want to be the Sugar Plum Fairy. I don't even want to be in the stupid show." So much for sounding calm. My voice gets higher and louder with every word.

Brenda looks skeptical. Epatha snorts.

"*Everyone* wants to be the Sugar Plum Fairy," Terrel says.

That does it. "*I* don't!" I yell. "How many times do I have to tell you? Doesn't anybody in New York have ears?"

Epatha's jaw drops open. I yank off my ballet slippers, put on my sneakers, and storm out the door.

Chapter 9

Mama's waiting on the steps under a bright blue umbrella.

"I hate ballet. I hate Harlem. Can we move back to Georgia?" I ask.

"What's the matter, baby?" she asks, putting her arm around my shoulders and pulling me under the umbrella.

"I have to be the stupid Sugar Plum Fairy in our dance show." I stomp through a puddle and immediately regret it as the water oozes through my sneakers into my socks.

Mama's face lights up. "The Sugar Plum Fairy? That sounds like a big part."

"It is," I growl. I'll be standing out, just like she wants. But I'll stand out for getting so dizzy I spin off the stage or for throwing up or something—probably not what Mama dreamed of.

"Well, that's wonderful, Alexandrea!"

"It is *not* wonderful. I can't do it. There are lots of turns, and I just about killed three people when we did turns practice."

"Now, sweetie. I'm sure they gave you the part because you're the best dancer. Ms. Debbé knows what she's doing."

"They drew my name out of a *hat*!" I yell.

"That is enough, Alexandrea Petrakova," Mama says.

"Fine," I mutter.

Mama stops walking and turns to face me. "Did you mean, 'yes, ma'am'?"

"No one says 'ma'am' around here," I tell

her. "I'm enough of a freak already. I dance like a freak. Do I have to talk like one, too?"

Being grounded is different in Harlem. In Georgia, it meant I couldn't go outside and play with my friends. Here I'm not supposed to go out by myself anyway, so Mama had to think of something different. So being grounded means I have to stay in my room. Luckily, I have a tiny TV in my room. Unluckily, being grounded also means Mama takes my TV away and puts it in her work-room. That way, she says, I'll have plenty of time to think about what I've done.

After an hour, I go into her workroom. She looks up from her sewing machine.

"I'm sorry I was disrespectful." I quickly add, "Ma'am."

"Thank you for your apology, Alexandrea." She hands me back my TV.

I sit on a stool beside her.

"Do I really have to take ballet? I want to be a speed skater, not a ballet dancer."

Mama looks at me. "Alexandrea, this is a whole new start for both of us. I want to make sure you don't miss any opportunities. We both have so much potential here in New York."

Potential again. If there does happen to be a tiny speck of potential in me somewhere, maybe I can have it surgically removed so everyone will leave me alone.

Mama sees me roll my eyes. She sighs. "I'll tell you what. You take the class till December. Really give it a chance, Alexandrea. It's important to me. If you still want to quit then, well . . ." She holds up her hands.

"Really?" I say. "I can?"

She nods.

"Thank you!" I put down the TV and jump into her arms.

"You have to give it your best shot, though. Deal?"

"Deal."

I skip down the hall to my room and plug in the TV. When I flip through the channels, I find a new show, *Swan Lake Smackdown*, where celebrities try to perform ballet dances.

This cheers me up. I may be bad, but these guys are terrible. A rock star clomps around like an elephant stuck in taffy. A famous football player flies into the air and falls over when he tries to do a chassé, which is kind of like a gallop. I laugh at them—until I think about the people who will be laughing at me when I try to do the Sugar Plum Fairy dance. Suddenly it's not so funny anymore.

I turn off the TV. Surely when the teachers see how bad I am, they'll give the part to some other kid. They wouldn't let me screw up the whole show.

Would they?

Chapter 10

When I walk into the waiting room before the next class, Epatha, Terrel, and Brenda are sitting together. Brenda says something—which, of course, I don't understand—and they all look at me. No one says hi. Okay, maybe I shouldn't have yelled at them. But *they* shouldn't have gotten all snippy about me being the Sugar Plum Fairy. I sit down on the bench farthest from them.

In class, we go through our barre exercises—*pliés*, *relevés*, *grand battements*. We move to the middle of the room to do floor work. I still struggle to keep up, but at least now I've seen all the moves before.

Halfway through class, Ms. Debbé says it's

time for us to start working on our dances. We split up into two groups. Ms. Debbé stays in the studio with the raindrops and the animals. Mr. Lester leads the monsters and me to one of the other classrooms.

The monsters are up first. Mr. Lester explains their dance to them. "You all know how little kids are scared of monsters in their closets, right?"

Jerzey Mae's eyes open wide. I'll bet she's *still* scared of monsters in her closet.

"For this dance, a Ballet One girl will be in a bed onstage. You'll come out of the closet and do a funny dance. She'll watch you, then chase you back into the closet. Got it?"

He shows them the first part of the dance, how they'll come in the door and gather around the bed to wake the little girl up. Then the girls line up and try it themselves.

Terrel and Epatha are really good dancers. Terrel does every move perfectly, like a windup doll. She gets all the steps right away. Epatha is good, too, but in a different way. She's wilder, with big jumps and big arm movements. She bugs her eyes out and makes scary faces. She really does look like a monster.

The triplets are the most interesting to watch. Jessica walks a little funny, but she dances well even with her special shoe. JoAnn, the skateboarder, picks up the steps almost as fast as Terrel.

But Jerzey Mae is a mess. She goes right when she's supposed to go left. She goes left when she's supposed to go right. JoAnn rolls her eyes and ignores her. Jessica tries to help, pointing her in the right direction when she messes up.

They go over the first part of the dance a few times. "Good work, girls," Mr. Lester says. He turns to me. "Your turn, Alexandrea."

My stomach clenches into a tight little ball. Fabulous—I get to make a fool of myself in front of a bunch of girls that hate me *and* a famous ballet director.

"You've heard of the ballet *The Nutcracker*?"

I nod. Mama makes me watch the DVD every Christmas. I always sit in front of her so I can take a little snooze without her knowing.

"There's a Sugar Plum Fairy in that who does a really flashy dance."

I must look as worried as I feel, because he laughs and adds, "Your dance isn't nearly that hard, I promise. But it uses the same music. Okay?"

Stalling seems like a good idea at this point. "Isn't that supposed to be a grown-up dance?"

Mr. Lester smiles. "Good point. When Ms. Debbé was a girl, she always wanted to dance the Sugar Plum Fairy, but the part always went to an adult. Now that she has her own school, a Ballet Three girl always gets to do a Sugar Plum Fairy dance."

"But why is it in summer?" I ask. I look at

the clock. If I can keep him talking for twelve more minutes, I'm home free.

"Lots of our girls dance in an adult dance company's *Nutcracker*, so it's hard for us to have a show during the holidays. So we put the Sugar Plum dance in our summer program." He raises an eyebrow. "Any other questions?"

He's on to me. I shake my head.

"So. You'll wear a beautiful, glittery, white dress—your mama will like that part— and do your dance to start off the Ballet Three program. Got it? Let's go."

I hope the other girls will leave, but they sit down on the floor to watch. Epatha folds her arms across her chest.

Mr. Lester shows me how I'll start off, frozen in the center of the stage with my arms spread out, a fairy wand in one hand. I can do that. I can't do turns, but I'm a genius at standing still.

Then I'm supposed to chassé to the left.

Then I chassé to the right. Mr. Lester shows me. I follow along behind him. So far, so good.

"Now you do four chaîné turns to the left," he says. He backs up and moves way across the room. Clearly he remembers how well I turn.

I turn once. I turn twice. I turn three times. I keel over.

Epatha whispers something to Brenda. My cheeks get hot. I pull myself up and try not to look at my ex-friends.

"Are you really spotting, Alexandrea?" Mr. Lester asks.

Well, I'm trying to. And there are definitely spots in front of my eyes. I nod yes.

"Hmmm," he says, rubbing his chin. "We'll need to work on that. Let's move on."

By the time class ends, we've gotten through the first part of my dance. Every time we reach a place where there are turns, I get dizzy and mess up.

"Hmmm," Mr. Lester says, rubbing his

beard again. "That's enough for today, girls. Go home and practice."

The other girls get up. Everyone ignores me except Jessica. She gives me a little smile, not in a nasty way but as if she feels bad for me. Maybe since her leg is messed up she knows what it's like not to be able to do things exactly right.

Each class after that, we spend a half hour all together doing our barre exercises and practicing moves. Then we split up to work on our dances. The monsters are always first. Their dance looks a little better every time they practice.

"Good work, Jerzey Mae," Mr. Lester calls out. Even she's getting better.

I am not getting better. I'm getting worse.

I still can't do turns. I can do the steps with Mr. Lester, but when I'm dancing alone I forget them. If I notice the other girls looking at me, I get nervous and make even more mistakes.

"Hmmm," Mr. Lester says over and over. He rubs his chin so much I'm surprised it's still on his face.

I try to practice at home. But how am I supposed to practice if I can't remember the steps?

I need to do turns in a straight line, so I try doing them in our hallway. I crash into one wall, then the other. When I knock a picture off the wall, Mama finally snaps at me: "What on earth are you doing, Alexandrea?"

"I gotta practice for my ballet show," I tell her.

She grumbles, but doesn't say anything else. She's been in a bad mood lately. Costume orders are not pouring in after all. There may be lots of theaters in New York, but it turns out there are lots of costume-makers here, too. I hear her whispering on the phone to Aunt Jackie at night. When I ask if we can fly home to Apple Creek for a visit, she says we can't be spending money on things we don't need right now. But then she tells me that worrying about money is her job, not mine. Which is good, because worrying about the recital is taking up all of my worry brain cells.

Saturday is especially bad. Mr. Lester tells me to go through my dance right from the start. I stand still at the beginning, the way I'm supposed to. Then I make the mistake of opening my eyes and seeing all the other girls reflected in the mirror, sitting in a row along the wall staring at me. My mind goes blank. I can't remember anything. I just stand there.

Mr. Lester turns the music off. "I would like to speak with Alexandrea alone," he tells the other girls. They file out of the room, sneaking looks back at me as they go.

"Alexandrea, I'm wondering if having you do the Sugar Plum Fairy dance is a good idea," Mr. Lester says. "Do you think you're going to be able to learn it?"

My eyes start to prickle. I blink hard. "I don't know," I say.

He looks at me kindly. "Why don't you think about it and tell me Tuesday. Talk to your mom about it. If you don't want to do it, we can find something else for you to do in the show. Maybe instead of having a Ballet One girl in the bed for the Monster Dance, it can be you."

I turn this over in my mind. Everyone in the whole school would know that I'd had to give up the Sugar Plum Fairy part because I was a terrible dancer. They'd all laugh at me. Mama would be so disappointed. She brought the Sugar Plum Fairy outfit home and sewed it up so it fit me perfectly. She even replaced some of the old lace and sequins.

But if I do the dance, I'll make an even bigger fool of myself. Would Mama rather have a daughter who was a coward, or one who embarrassed herself in front of an auditorium full of people?

"I'll think about it," I tell Mr. Lester. But I've already made up my mind. I just need to find a way to tell Mama.

Chapter 11

When I meet Mama after class, she's carrying three shopping bags full of fabric. She's in a great mood, because she finally found someone who needs some flashy dresses. It's a man who dresses up like a woman and sings show tunes in a theater. Mama's never made a dress for a man before, but she doesn't care. "Man, woman, crocodile, whatever—someone wants a dress and has the money, I'll make it," she says as we walk down 125th Street past the Apollo Theater. "Plus, this fellow understands what it means to make a theatrical statement."

We stop in and pick up a pizza to celebrate. She hums as she sprinkles red pepper flakes on her slice. I can't bring myself to tell her I'm a Sugar Plum reject. Maybe later.

After dinner she heads right to her workroom. She sings at the top of her lungs, and I can hear her sewing machine clattering away. I'll tell her tomorrow.

I turn on my little TV and channel surf. A basketball game, a dumb cartoon, and a game show . . . and there's *Swan Lake Smackdown* again.

I recognize a soap opera star leaping across the stage in tights. The lady he's dancing with looks nervous. I wonder how many times he's stomped on her toes. I'm about to change channels when I see a familiar face. The camera closes in on a woman with creamy coffee skin, short dark hair, and clear green eyes.

I don't believe it. It's Phoebe Fitz, my speed skating idol. Doing ballet. She and her partner spin side by side over and over. She looks like she's having fun. The audience loves her.

After the dance, a man in a tuxedo talks to her. "Wonderful job, Phoebe—but ballet must be quite different from speed skating, right?"

"They're not as different as you'd think. Ballet's about balance and rhythm and timing. You gotta be strong, and you gotta be fast. I'm going to make the kids I coach take it."

I flip off the TV and sit on the edge of my bed, stunned.

Well, okay. If Phoebe Fitz thinks I should do ballet, I will. I won't give up. I will give the Sugar Plum thing my very best shot.

But I'm going to need lots of help.

Chapter 12

I get to ballet class early on Saturday. Terrel's stretching, her leg propped up on the trash can. Epatha is lying on a bench admiring the shiny pink heart stickers on her fingernails. Brenda has another 5,000-page book of body parts on her lap.

I walk over to them. Epatha sits up. Terrel stops stretching. Brenda closes the book, sticking her finger in it to keep her place.

I take a deep breath. "I'm sorry I yelled at you guys. I was mad. My mom is not dating Mr. Lester. And I did not want to get that part. But I got it anyway. And I am terrible."

Terrel nods in agreement. "You *are* terrible. No offense."

Epatha squirms around on the bench. "We shouldn't have gotten mad at you, I guess. You got the part fair and square. Mr. Lester wouldn't have rigged the drawing."

I go on. "You guys are the best dancers in the class."

Epatha puffs out her cheeks and smiles a little.

"I'm not," says Brenda. "JoAnn's better than I am."

"You're still good," I say quickly. "And you're really smart. I need you all to help me learn my dance so I don't wreck the whole show. Please?"

They're quiet for a minute. My heart pounds in my chest.

"Well . . ." Epatha says. She looks at Terrel and Brenda. They nod.

"We'd have to practice outside of class," Epatha says. "Where do you live?"

I tell her.

"That's around the corner from me," she says. "And Terrel is down the street. There's a storage room in the back of our restaurant we can practice in. Everyone, come over tomorrow afternoon, okay?"

The lump in my stomach dissolves. "Thanks," I say.

The next afternoon Mama drops me off at Bella Italia, the restaurant Epatha's family owns. Epatha leads me past crowded red booths and through the noisy kitchen into a back room. Huge cans of tomato sauce and boxes of pasta line the shelves on one wall. The smell of warm lasagna and garlic bread leaks under the door and tickles my nose.

Terrel comes in carrying a boom box and a CD. "The triplets' dad had the Sugar Plum Fairy music. I borrowed it," she says.

Brenda arrives with a stack of books. This time the books aren't about blood vessels or bones; they're about ballet.

Terrel calls us to attention. "Alexandrea has three problems. She can't do spins. She does not dance with feeling and emotion. And—"

I interrupt. "How can I dance with feeling and emotion if I can't do the steps?"

"Exactly," Terrel continues. "And she does not know the steps."

"*Muchos problemas,*" Epatha says to me. "That's a lot of problems, girl."

I already *know* all this. "So, how are we going to fix them?" I ask Terrel, trying not to whine.

"I know all the steps from watching Mr. Lester try to teach you," Terrel says. "I'll help you learn them. Epatha dances with lots of feeling. She'll help you with that. And Brenda will figure out why you can't do turns."

I'm impressed. Terrel is like a military commander going into battle. I start to feel like it might not be hopeless after all.

"Brenda, you're first," Terrel says.

Brenda looks up from the book she's reading. "Right. Spins," she says. "Watch I'll. Turn chaîné one do, Al. Okay."

I think she's telling me to do a chaîné turn. I stand with my arms out to my sides. I step across with one leg, turn my body around, and end up a few feet away.

Brenda squints and refers back to her book. "Bad not actually is technique your," she begins.

Terrel interrupts. "Brenda, talk forward so she can understand you. We've got enough problems."

Brenda sighs, as if talking forward for five minutes is going to ruin her mental development. "Okay. Your technique is actually not bad. Use your arms more, though. They'll help pull you around."

It's nice to understand Brenda for a change. I try again.

"Are you really spotting?" she asks.

"I can't," I say. "I just don't get it."

"You can't just look at the whole wall. You need to focus *really hard* on one little place. Or one thing, like . . ." She looks around. She picks up a bright red jar of marinated mushrooms and holds it in the air. "Look at the mushrooms," she says. "No, look at this *one* mushroom." She points to one mushroom smashed up against the glass of the jar.

I do.

"Now, slowly do a turn," Brenda continues. "Keep looking at the mushroom as long as you can."

I stare hard at the mushrooms. I turn my body. At the last minute, I whip my head around and look at the can again.

"Now, faster," Brenda says.

I turn once, twice, three times, my eyes burning into the can. I crash into a crate of macaroni at the end of the room. But only because I wasn't looking where I was going, not because I felt dizzy.

"You dizzy?" Brenda asks.

I push myself upright and shake my head to check. "No!" I say. "I'm not!"

We practice until I can turn without knocking over any pasta boxes.

"Brava, bellissima!" Epatha calls. She comes over and high-fives me. "Nice work, Brenda," she says, high-fiving her, too. Brenda smiles modestly.

"One problem down," Terrel says. "Two to go."

Chapter 13

We meet at the restaurant almost every day. Sometimes Terrel and one of her brothers pick me up, and sometimes Mama walks me over. One day a man stops Mama on the street and asks where the Apollo Theater is. I tell him before Mama can even open her mouth.

"You're turning into a real New Yorker!" she says afterward. I can tell she's proud of me.

In the restaurant storage room, Terrel works with me on my steps. She teaches me a tiny little part of the dance and makes me do it again and again. Then she hooks it up to the little tiny part that comes before, and we practice it all together.

Brenda drills me on my turns. Every day she holds up a different food package for me to stare at as I spin around. "We don't want you to get conditioned so you can only spin if you're looking at marinated mushrooms," she explains. So I do tortellini twirls, spaghetti spins, and rigatoni rotations.

Once I have the steps, Epatha helps me put some personality into them. Instead of a chassé, she does a chassé with attitude. I try to copy her.

"Don't do it like me," she says. "You gotta do it like *you*. Find your inner Sugar Plum Fairy."

What *is* a Sugar Plum Fairy, anyway? I decide she must be kind of like the tooth fairy. I close my eyes and imagine I *am* the Sugar Plum Fairy. I'm beautiful. I live in a castle. I toss candy bars onto kids' pillows while they sleep. Maybe the tooth fairy follows behind me to collect the teeth the kids lose in caramel bars.

"Now you're getting it," Epatha says with satisfaction. "You ain't just doing the steps. You're dancing."

She and Brenda and Terrel do the dance with me. Epatha stands on my left, and Terrel and Brenda on my right. When we're dancing together, I don't get nervous. I don't forget the steps. It's actually . . . I can't believe it . . . *fun*.

Mr. Lester is astonished at my progress. "Wonderful work, Alexandrea!" he calls out in the middle of my dance. I still forget the steps sometimes, but Terrel watches from the sidelines and gives me little hints or points me in the right direction.

Epatha, Brenda, Terrel, and I hang out at the restaurant all the time. Epatha's parents are cool. Instead of sticking their noses into the storage room every two seconds the way some parents would, they leave us alone. When we're done, we sit in one of the booths in the back. Nonna—Epatha's squat Italian grandma, who always wears a black dress, a white apron, and black knee-high stockings—brings over big plates of spaghetti for us.

"Much better than Puerto Rican food," she says, glaring across the room at Abuela, Epatha's other grandma.

"Mm-hmmm," says Epatha.

Tall, elegant Abuela—Epatha's Puerto Rican grandma—makes us flan; little mounds of custard with caramel on top. "Much better than Italian food," she says, winking at us.

"You bet," says Epatha. The rest of us just smile and eat everything up.

The triplets come over sometimes to practice the Monster Ballet with Epatha, Brenda, and Terrel. Then they hang out to watch my dance. They've started to pick up the steps, too, even Jerzey Mae.

Sometimes when there are no customers, the waiters come into the back to watch us. If I notice them watching, my stomach fills up with butterflies, and I freeze. I can't remember any of the steps.

After this happens for the third time, Terrel sighs. "I think we got a fourth problem," she says. "Stage fright." She looks at Brenda.

"It on I'm," Brenda says.

Brenda and Terrel come into the Nutcracker School the next day smiling. "Underwear," Brenda says.

"What?" Epatha asks.

"The solution to Al's problem," says Terrel.

"I already *wear* underwear," I say defensively.

They sit down on the bench with us. "Al has to think about underwear," says Terrel.

Brenda holds up a book called *Stop Stage Fright*.

Epatha whistles. "*Un libro para todo.* Girl, you find a book for everything."

Brenda opens the book, holds it under my nose, and points to a spot. I read out loud, *"One way to cure stage fright is to pretend everyone in the audience is sitting there in their underwear. It is quite difficult to be scared of people in underwear."*

"They ain't seen Nonna in her zebra-stripe

slip," Epatha says. "Now, *that's* scary."

But I have to admit that the underwear trick is worth a shot.

The next time the waiters watch us dance, I imagine fat old Alfredo standing there in red long underwear. I picture Fabio, who has a long mustache and is always flirting with lady customers, in shiny pink boxer shorts with hearts on them.

It works! I can hardly dance, because I'm laughing so hard, but I don't forget any of the steps.

"Underwear," I tell the other girls. They look at Alfredo and Fabio. We all crack up.

"*Ragazze pazze*—crazy girls. Always giggling over nothing." Fabio throws his hands in the air.

Epatha's mom comes in, brushing the flour off her hands. Her apron has bright green parrots on it, and her dark, wavy hair is clipped back with a shiny pink, green, and orange clip. You can tell where Epatha gets her style.

"Girls, the restaurant inspector is coming next Friday," she says. "We want to get this room cleaned up. I'm sorry, but you'll need to find somewhere else to practice next week."

"We can't do it at my house," Terrel says. "My brothers would get in the way." She has five older brothers, which is probably why she's so good at bossing people around.

"Place my to come can you," Brenda says.

"Her apartment?" I ask.

Epatha nods. "It's kind of small, but we can dance small."

We all say good-bye in the front of the restaurant. Mama lets me walk home alone from Epatha's, since it's just a block from our apartment. The air is crisp, and the late after-noon sun is turning the sky orange. I crunch through a pile of dead leaves on the sidewalk. Someone's eating fried chicken and waffles in a booth by the window of the soul food restaurant. You don't find chicken and waffles in Apple Creek, that's for sure.

All the street noise that used to keep me awake at night and make me jittery during the day seems exciting now. All these people going all these places. I pass the old guys playing checkers on the corner, as always. One of them smiles at me and tips his hat. I wave.

I walk up the creaky stairs to our apartment. I'm not even scared of them the way I used to be. But I am scared of what I see when I open our door.

Moving boxes.

Chapter 14

Mama comes out of her workroom when she hears the door creak open. Her eyes are puffy. She follows my gaze to the moving boxes stacked against the living room wall.

"I think we may need to go back to Georgia after all, Alexandrea."

"What do you mean, go back?" I ask. "We've only been here two months."

But I know that except for the dresses she made for that guy, she hasn't found any other costume jobs, even though she's been going around to lots of theaters and dance places. She says you need personal connections, which means people you know making their friends hire you.

"You can't just give up!" I tell her. "You told me not to give up on ballet. You said we had lots of potential here."

She sits down on the couch and pats the place beside her. I sit down. When we first moved here, I never thought this apartment would feel like home. But now it does. This couch fits perfectly under the windows. The ceramic handprint I made in kindergarten is hanging on the wall. I've even gotten used to my ballet-nightmare room.

"I want to be straight with you, Alexandrea. I thought I'd planned everything out, but I didn't realize how expensive New York is. And I'd hoped the business would take off faster."

She brushes my hair out of my eyes. "Fact is, it hasn't. And I don't know what else to do."

"But, Mama . . . can't you get some other kind of job for a while? Our ballet show's in two weeks—we don't have to go before then, do we?"

"If we have to move, I want to get you back

before school starts. And you know no one's bought my shop in Apple Creek yet, so I can get it back." The light seems to go out of her eyes as she says this. "But you'll be with your old friends again—that'll be nice, won't it?"

I think about Keisha and my other friends from Apple Creek. I miss them, kind of, but my life there seems as if it happened a long time ago.

Then I think about Epatha talking in three languages at once. And Terrel ordering us around. And Brenda, who can find anything anyone needs in a book. And the way they've all helped me learn my dance.

"Mama, I really want to stay now. Please?"

She looks at me for a long time. "We'll stay till your show's done. After that, unless something changes . . ."

She doesn't need to finish her sentence. I stuff the moving boxes back into the closet and give them a good hard kick.

Chapter 15

On Sunday afternoon, Terrel's big brother, Cheng, takes us to the park. He has some really old roller skates that fit Terrel if she sticks cotton in the toes, so I told her I'd teach her to skate. Cheng hangs out on a bench with his friends while I show Terrel how to lace up the skates just right. After all the time she spent going over the dance with me, it feels good that I can finally show her something.

Terrel stands up. The right skate starts wheeling right, and the left one starts wheeling left. I grab her before she falls on her rear—good thing her brother has a helmet we can use, too.

"I guess this is how you felt when you were

learning the Sugar Plum dance," she pants, after falling over for the fifth time.

When she's had enough skating for the day, it's my turn. I tie on the skates. They're a perfect fit. Terrel sits on a bench while I race up and down the sidewalk. I see an older lady wearing a huge feathered hat on the sidewalk across the street.

"That's the lady who picks you up after class sometimes, right?" I ask Terrel.

Terrel nods. "It's my grandma. She must be coming back from church."

"That's quite a hat," I say.

"All the ladies at her church wear big hats," Terrel replies. "They call them crowns. It's like they try to out-hat each other. Grandma has at least twenty of them, and she buys more whenever she goes to a church convention."

It feels like puzzle pieces are floating around in my brain but they're not fitting together yet.

"Where does she buy them?" I ask.

"She used to get them at a place called Emma's Crowns, but Emma got old and went to Florida. Grandma says there're no really good hat shops around anymore."

The puzzle pieces snap into place.

"Let's meet at my apartment on Monday instead of Brenda's," I say. "And have your grandma come pick you up after."

"Why?" Terrel asks.

"You'll see."

Chapter 16

On Monday afternoon, Mama runs down to the store to get snacks for us to have after we practice. While she's gone, I move all the hats she's made from the workroom out to the living room. I set them on their hat stands, too, so it looks like a bunch of fancy, faceless ladies are perched around the edge of the room.

"What are all my hats doing out?" Mama asks, as she shuts the door and puts away her handbag.

I think fast. "We need an audience so it feels more like we're performing."

"Well, don't knock them over," she says.

All the girls show up at our apartment at

the same time. I introduce Mama to everyone.

"Wow—you look like a model," Epatha says. "What a cool outfit."

Cool is right—it's the Iceberg Suit. My friends all walk around Mama and admire the shimmering fabric.

"I wish my mom had a suit like that," Brenda says.

Mama brushes off their compliments, but I can tell she's pleased.

"Can I watch you ladies practice?" she asks me.

I get nervous thinking about her watching, and I do not want to have to picture my Mama in underwear. "No—I want it to be a surprise," I tell her.

After we go through my dance, and then the Monster Dance for good measure, we have some cookies and juice. Then Epatha asks if we can see Mama's workroom.

"Sure," I tell her.

We go back, and Epatha heads straight to the costume rack. "Wow," she says. "Wow, wow, wow." She goes right to an orange dress with feathers and a matching headpiece. "This is totally me."

Mama smiles. "Let's see how it looks." She takes the dress, leads Epatha to the mirror, and holds it in front of her. "I think you're right—that dress *is* you."

Meanwhile, Brenda is looking with interest at the drawers of sequins.

"You make all those hats out front?" Terrel asks Mama.

"Yes," Mama says. "I mostly do costumes, but I like hats, too."

Terrel gives me a big grin. "Now I know why you wanted to practice over here," she whispers.

Epatha calls me over to admire her. Pretty soon we're all parading around the room in different costumes and hats. Mama even talks Brenda into trying on a black-and-white dress with a big, triangle-shaped collar.

"Up-dress playing of think would Vinci da Leonardo what know don't I," says Brenda.

"*What* did she say?" Mama whispers to Terrel.

"She says she doesn't know what Leonardo da Vinci would think of playing dress-up," Terrel tells Mama.

"Well, he's been dead for about a million years, so we ain't gonna tell him," says Epatha.

The doorbell rings. Mama calls down on the intercom. "Who is it?"

"Mahalia Ducket, Terrel's grandma," a voice crackles through the speaker.

Mama buzzes her up.

The door opens, and Mrs. Ducket comes in. She's tiny with dark brown skin, like

124

Terrel. She has crooked teeth, like Terrel. She marches right over to one of the hat stands, moving exactly like a bigger version of Terrel.

"My goodness," she says. "Where did these lovely hats come from?"

"My mama makes them," I say. "She sells them, too."

Mrs. Ducket goes from hat stand to hat stand. She picks up some of the hats. We all watch in silence. Mama looks as if she can't quite figure out what's happening.

"May I try these on?" Mrs. Ducket asks.

"Uh . . . of course," Mama says. "I'll get you a mirror."

Mrs. Ducket tries on a pink hat with netting and a huge cloth hydrangea on top. She tries on a black hat with squares of silver netting that dangle down. She tries on the orange and purple hat that looks like an ostrich's rear end.

"I'll take them," she says.

"Which?" Mama asks, a little dazed.

"All three," Mrs. Ducket says. "The ladies at my church wear fancy hats. We buy *lots* of hats. And these are one-of-a-kind. How much?"

Mama pauses. I don't know if she's even thought about how much to charge.

Mrs. Ducket opens her purse, takes out a stack of bills, and hands them to Mama. "Okay?"

Mama's eyes get big. She nods.

"I'll pick them up tomorrow," says Mrs. Ducket. "Can you make more? If you can, I'll bring some of my friends by. But let me tell you something," she says, leaning closer to Mama. "You should charge them twice as much. These hats are worth it." She winks, turns briskly, and marches out the door.

Mama throws her arms around Terrel. "Your grandma may have just saved our skins." She looks at me. "You put those hats out there to be an audience, did you?"

"Yes, ma'am," I say, grinning. She gives me a big hug, too, and twirls me around in the air.

The doorbell rings. Mrs. Ducket comes back upstairs.

"Did you forget something?" Mama asks.

"Yes," Mrs. Ducket says. She takes Terrel by the hand and pulls her out the door.

Chapter 17

Before we know it, it's the weekend before the show.

Ballet One, Ballet Two, and Ballet Three classes all share one program, so everyone from kindergartners to fourth graders comes to the ballet school on Saturday to get costumes. One studio has been turned into a costume room. Mama volunteered to help out (which is why the giraffe is chocolate brown with shimmering gold spots and the elephant wears an exotic hat). A few other harried moms measure kids and pull costumes off the racks for them. They also sew the costumes back together when the kids wreck them, which is usually about two minutes after they put them on.

"Kitties, hold your tails up!" one of the moms yells. "And try not to step on them!" A circle of tailless cats surround her, waving tails that need to be sewn back on. The Ballet Two teacher finally decides the cats will be Manx cats.

On the other side of the room, Tiara Girl is struggling to get into her warthog suit. She has to wear a big papier-mâché warthog head with bristly ears and big tusks. I wonder if they make warthog-size tiaras. I smile and wave at her. She glowers back.

Epatha, Brenda, Terrel, and the triplets get their furry monster costumes. The costumes look even more like hairy grapes in person than they did in the drawing. Jerzey Mae looks miserable. She sidles over to the rack where my fairy costume is hanging and runs a finger gently along a row of sequins.

"You want to try it on?" I ask. I help her into it. "The Monster Ballet is really cute," I say, as she admires herself in the mirror.

"At least no one can see it's me inside the suit," she says.

Mama's racing around like crazy, pinning and sewing. She's on her knees adjusting the giraffe's tail when I see Mr. Lester and Ms. Debbé come in. Mr. Lester leads Ms. Debbé over to Mama and taps Mama on the back.

"Mom, I'd like you to meet Yolanda Johnson. She's been doing a great job for us making some new costumes and reworking the old ones."

Mama's eyes get big as Ms. Debbé extends her hand. For a minute I'm afraid Mama might kiss it, like someone would kiss a king's hand in an old movie. But Mama pulls herself together and shakes Ms. Debbé's hand.

"The costumes, they look simply wonderful," Ms. Debbé says. "You have much talent."

Mama looks like she's about to pass out.

"Ms. Johnson is starting a costume business," Mr. Lester says.

"Really?" says Ms. Debbé. "Please see that I get some of your business cards. I will tell my friends about you."

Ms. Debbé sweeps out of the room. Mr. Lester follows her. On his way out, he gives me a wink.

Mama, for the first time in her life, is totally speechless.

The show's set for next Saturday night. On Friday afternoon, we have a dress rehearsal up in the big studio. It looks like a real theater. There's a stage at one end, with big red and black curtains on the side. There are lots of chairs set up for the audience. A guy stands on a ladder messing with some spotlights.

"No luck," he says to Ms. Debbé, who is hovering next to him. "The circuit's not working."

"We must have lights for the show!" Ms. Debbé says. "It is essential!"

"Don't worry, you'll have your lights," he says. One of the dancing cats chases another, then clobbers her, nearly knocking over the ladder.

"I'll come back after all these . . . uh, precious little girls are gone," the lighting guy says.

Meanwhile, Mr. Lester tries to organize the Ballet Three girls while two of the other teachers wrangle the littler kids. "Monsters over here! Animals there! Raindrops, by the back wall!"

He tells us we'll wait quietly—he emphasizes *quietly*—in the studio across the hall till he comes to get each group. We'll stand backstage until the applause for the previous number finishes; then we'll go on and do our dances.

"All except you, Al," he says. "You'll be

right after intermission. The monsters will wait backstage for your dance to end."

"Quiet, everyone!" Ms. Debbé raps her walking stick for attention. "Our dress rehearsal is beginning!"

We get to sit and watch the little kids dance, since we won't be able to see them tomorrow.

I sit between Brenda and Epatha in the third row. The Ballet One kids are all dressed like little yellow flowers. Their teacher dances with them, but one flower still wanders off the stage in the middle of the dance. Another sits down in the center of the stage and starts bawling. One starts singing, *"Row, row, row your boat,"* at the top of her lungs. When we laugh, she looks pleased and sings even louder. The teacher smiles as if she couldn't be happier that these kids are wrecking her dance. Mr. Lester finally comes on, scoops up the singer and the crier, and carries them offstage.

Some of the Ballet Two girls are doing a princess dance. They all have pink, fluffy dresses and crowns.

"Everyone gets to look nice except us," I hear Jerzey Mae whisper behind me.

"Maybe you'll get to be a princess next year," Jessica says soothingly.

"Princess, shmincess," JoAnn says. "Why can't we do a skateboard dance?"

We watch the princesses, then the dancing tailless cats. After their dance ends, Mr. Lester leads all the Ballet Three girls out of the audience and across the hall. "Animals and raindrops, stay here," he says. "Alexandrea, you and the monsters follow me."

We go back into the studio by a side door so we're hidden from the audience. I hear the little kids thumping into the seats to watch us.

"Monsters, wait backstage—you can watch Alexandrea's dance from the wings. When it's almost over, prepare to come on. Alexandrea, take your place in the center of the stage. The curtain will open. When you're ready, look at me and I'll start the music."

I go to the middle of the stage. It feels lonely and big. I stretch my arms out like I'm supposed to. I hear ropes creaking, and the curtain opens slowly. My stomach flutters.

Suddenly I'm looking out on the roomful of kids. There are millions of them. My mind goes blank. What am I doing up here? I can't remember the first step. I can't even remember my own name!

"Psst!" Brenda whispers from the wings. "Underwear!"

I look out and choose a girl in the front row. I imagine her in underwear instead of her yellow flower outfit. She's not so scary. I imagine rows and rows of kids in goofy underwear.

Chassé left! That's the first step. I nod to Mr. Lester. He starts the music.

My dance goes just fine after that. When I'm done, I curtsy the way Mr. Lester showed me, then go off to the wings to watch the monsters. Even Jerzey Mae does well.

When they come off, Epatha gives me a hug. "Nice work, Sugar Plum Fairy," she says.

"Nice work, monsters," I reply.

Ms. Debbé comes backstage and kisses both of my cheeks. "*Fantastique!* You see? All students have potential. It was easy, yes?"

Epatha, Terrel, Brenda, and I exchange looks.

"It was easy, no," I say.

"Tomorrow will be a piece of cake," Mr. Lester says. "That's why we have dress rehearsals like this—so there won't be any surprises the night of the show."

But Mr. Lester is wrong.

Chapter 18

"Hurry up, Mama," I say. She's been messing with my hair forever. "We gotta get there by seven o'clock."

"I know when we gotta get there, Miss Sugar Plum Fairy," she says, putting another little white sparkly flower into my hair. "Almost done."

After three more snaps, she steps back to admire her work. She turns me around to face the mirror. "Does your mama rock, or what?"

The top of my white dress sparkles with all the new sequins Mama has added. Layer after airy layer of fabric floats around my hips. My hair is slicked back in a bun, with the flowers all over catching the light when I move.

"Yes, ma'am. You definitely rock," I reply.

"Nervous?" she asks.

"Why would I be nervous?" I ask. No need to be nervous when I have the underwear trick ready to go.

"That's right, baby," she says. "You all have been practicing so much that you can probably do that dance in your sleep."

She's right—I did the dance over and over in my dreams last night. Every step was right on. Nothing can go wrong now.

"Come on, Alexandrea—let's go get a cab," Mama says.

"A cab?" I say as she opens the door.

"Dance stars do *not* walk to the theater when they perform," she says. She waves her arm in the air when we get outside, and a taxi pulls right up in front of us.

I've never been in a cab before. I sit in the back with Mama. We race through traffic and get to the dance studio in no time at all. Mama hands the driver some money, then gives me a hug.

"Break a leg, baby," she says.

"What?" I shriek. That seems like a rotten thing to say to your daughter when she's about to do a dance.

She laughs. "It's theater talk. Show people think it's bad luck to say, 'good luck,' so they say, 'break a leg' instead."

"Oh." I walk up the stairs very carefully anyway.

After Mama goes to get a seat, I go to the studio where the Ballet Three girls are supposed to meet. Mr. Lester checks my name off his list. All the monsters are already here. Epatha waves me over. She grins at me through the face hole in her purple monster costume. Even her cheeks are purple.

"If you're going to be purple, you might as well be *all* purple," she says. "I used some of my mom's eye shadow."

"How long before we go on?" I ask.

"Minutes twenty about take dances kids' little the," says Brenda.

I'm too nervous even to try to figure that one out. I look at Terrel.

"If the little kids take twenty minutes, we're probably on at eight," she says.

A whole hour.

"You guys scared?" I ask.

"Naaah," says Epatha.

Brenda raises her eyebrow. Epatha's foot is tapping as if she's trying to talk in Morse code.

"Well . . . a little," Epatha admits.

Soon we hear a burst of applause. The show must be starting. We can hear the flower dance music leaking under the door.

"Let's sneak out and see how many people are there," Epatha says.

Brenda, Terrel, and I follow her into the hallway. The door to the big studio is open a crack. Epatha peeks in.

"Mamma mia," she says. "That's one heck of a lot of people."

I look inside. The studio is totally jammed. Every single seat is filled. People are standing at the back and along the sides. There are even people sitting on the floor right in front of the stage. We overhear two of the moms talking to each other. "I counted over two hundred people—isn't that wonderful?" one of them says.

We walk silently back to the room.

"I didn't know there would be *that* many," Terrel says.

Now that I know how many people are out there, I decide I can wait a while to do my dance. In fact, I can wait forever.

But before we know it, it's intermission, and Mr. Lester is leading the monsters and me down the hallway.

"You'll all be wonderful, girls," he says reassuringly. I swallow hard. Maybe there will be a fire drill, and they'll stop the show. Maybe a UFO will crash into the roof. Maybe . . .

"Alexandrea, you're on," hc says. I don't move. He takes me by the shoulders and pushes me toward the stage. I can see the monsters lined up in the wings.

I stretch my arms out. Underwear, I think to myself. Underwear, underwear, underwear.

The ropes squeak, and the curtains part. A bright light hits me in the face like a fist. They got the lights fixed—but they're blinding me. I can't see out into the audience.

Applause fills the room. They're clapping for me. My stomach flips and flops. My mind goes blank. I can't remember anything except underwear.

How can I picture someone in underwear if I can't see the audience at all? I squint to try to make out a face, but all I see are blobs of black and the fierce shine of the lights pointing onstage. I start to panic.

I continue to stand there with my arms out. The audience stops clapping and waits expectantly.

I stand.

And stand.

Mr. Lester waits for me to look at him so he can start the music.

I will never remember the steps. I will be standing here onstage with everyone staring at me for the rest of my life. A drop of sweat rolls down the side of my face.

Then, out of the corner of my eye, I see something move. Something purple.

Epatha walks onstage. She plants herself to my left, just like she did when we practiced the dance together.

Terrel and Brenda come onstage, too. They stand on my right.

Even the triplets come on. They stand behind us.

Epatha nods to Mr. Lester. His eyes look a

little wild, but he starts the music.

"Let's do it, girlfriend," Epatha says.

The steps flood back into my head as the music starts. We chassé left, then right. It's just like all the times we practiced in the restaurant. I can almost smell the lasagna.

With my friends beside me, I jump like a gazelle and even spin, spin, spin like a real ballerina. The triplets do the dance, too, even though Jerzey Mae goes left one time she's supposed to go right. But it doesn't matter.

When we finish, the room explodes with applause. We line up, all together, and curtsy. *"Thank you,"* I whisper to all of my friends as I leave the stage. Epatha winks. Then they get into place for their dance.

After the show is over, we push our way past all the parents and friends back to our dressing room. We're behind a well-dressed man and lady. The lady says, "I loved the Sugar Plum Fairy's dance. But what were those purple things?"

"Those were the Sugar Plums," the man replies knowingly.

Epatha nudges me.

Mama comes in with Terrel's grandma and dad, Epatha's parents, Brenda's mom, and the triplets' mom and dad. They hug us all and tell us how great we were.

Mr. Lester appears while we're pulling on our jackets. "Not exactly what we'd planned, but very nice, girls. How did your friends learn your dance, Alexandrea?"

"We aren't just her friends," Epatha says. "We're her sisters."

"We are the Sugar Plum Sisters," says Terrel. She locks pinkies with Epatha, who locks them with Brenda, who locks them with JoAnn, who locks them with Jerzey Mae, who locks them with Jessica, who locks them with me.

"Sugar Plum Power!" Epatha says.

"Sugar Plum Power!" we all say.

Then we walk with our families out into the cool night air toward Bella Italia, where six extralarge pizzas are waiting for us.

Chapter 19

It's September eighth, my birthday, and we're down at the Chelsea Piers skating rink for my birthday party. Finally I'm gliding over the ice. My skates fly as I go around and around and around the rink.

"You're really good!" JoAnn says. "You should try skateboarding."

Mama gives her a look. "She should *not* try skateboarding."

Brenda nods. I hear her say, "Ice-skating is safer. When you fall, there's less friction. That means you glide instead of getting all ripped up. Although I did just read about how to sew people up with stitches."

"What did she say?" Mama asks, bewildered.

I stare at Brenda. "Did you say that forward or backward?"

She looks at me like I'm crazy. "Backward."

I can't believe it! I can finally understand Brenda. I grin so hard my cheeks hurt.

A lot's happened since the show. Mrs. Ducket showed off her hats to her friends, who told their friends. Mama's set up a hat shop next door to Aunt Jackie's hair salon. It's called Yolanda's Crowns for Urban Royalty. Mama can't make hats fast enough to keep up with business. She's even getting some costume jobs from friends of Ms. Debbé. That means we get to stay here. And I'm glad.

Mama smiles as I zoom around the rink. The triplets have never skated in their lives. JoAnn gets it fast, but Jerzey Mae and Jessica are clutching each other. Epatha's a natural, and Terrel's doing okay, too—I think the roller-skating might have helped.

I go to the edge for a breather. Mama comes over.

"You look really happy, birthday girl," she says.

"I am." I smile at her.

"I haven't forgotten our deal, Alexandrea. If you want to quit ballet and take skating, you can."

I look at my friends out on the ice. JoAnn's trying to spin. Brenda's calling out encouragement to her (backward!). Terrel's struggling to pull Jerzey Mae and Jessica up from the heap they've fallen into. Epatha skates over to Mama and me.

"Can I take skating *and* ballet?" I ask.

"I think we might be able to arrange that," Mama says. She gazes into the distance, then slams her hands down on the edge of the rink.

"Why didn't I think of this before?" she says. "You can be a figure skater! That way, you can skate *and* still wear beautiful costumes!

And I know exactly what outfit to make for your first competition. I'm seeing blue— electric-sky blue . . . more lightning bolts . . . maybe some feathers, to represent birds in flight . . ."

Epatha's eyes pop out in horror. I laugh. At least it's progress.

I grab Epatha's hand and pull her away. "Race you around the rink," I say. And we're off, ice shavings flying behind us.

Al's Guide to Ballet Terms

barre—the bar you hold on to in order to keep yourself from falling over when you're doing things like pliés.

chaîné turns—turns you do in a straight line or a circle unless you're terrible at them like I used to be. If you're like I was, you do a few, then crash into the wall.

chassé—step where you move across the floor with one foot chasing the other. It's kind of like a gallop, but gallop doesn't sound fancy enough for ballet.

first position—when your heels are together and your toes (or, as Brenda would say, your phalanges) stick out.

grand battement—big kick. If Tiara Girl's standing in front of me at the barre, I do these extra-big.

grand jeté—big leap across the floor. I'm
really good at these unless my tutu falls off.

plié—knee-bend. A **demi-plié** is a little one,
and a **grand plié** is a big one. Epatha adds
little jumps and flashy arm moves when Ms.
Debbé's not looking.

relevé—when you go up on your toes. When Terrel does this, she's almost as tall as the rest of us (unless we're doing it too; then she's out of luck).

spot—look hard at something (like a jar of marinated mushrooms) so you don't get dizzy while you're turning.

BOOK TWO

TOESHOE TROUBLE

Chapter 1

"Brenda?"

The voice sounds like it's far, far away. That's because I'm buried in what my friend Al calls one of my "body part" books. (The proper term is actually *anatomy*.) I get one from the library each week, since I want to be a doctor when I grow up. I'll need to learn every bone and muscle in the human body at some point, so I figure I might as well do it now. Plus, I'm only nine, and I want to get all the important information I can into my head early, so it'll sink in before my brain gets filled with ridiculous things like how to put on eye makeup and how to make boys like you.

I squint at a picture of a skull. I thought

the main part of your skull was just one big bone, but it turns out it's really a bunch of little bones that are all stuck together. Why is this? Wouldn't a big piece of bone be stronger? Motorcycle helmets are supposed to protect your brain, too, and they don't look like jigsaw puzzles.

A white-socked foot with a hole in the toe taps my leg. "Brenda!"

I surface. It's late afternoon on Sunday. Mom's at the other end of the couch. She's put down the book she was reading, and now she's poking me with her foot again.

"What?" I ask.

"Getting hungry?"

I nod. Sunday is my favorite day of the week, since Mom usually has to work on Saturdays. First, we have waffles for breakfast; then we go to a free museum or walk around Central Park. Afterward, we come home and read on the couch till it's time to make supper,

which on Sundays is always alphabet pasta with olives and artichoke hearts. Every week we see who can spell the longest words with her pasta. Mom knows lots more words than I do, but I know more disease names, like hemochromatosis and pneumoconiosis, so I can hold my own.

"Chocolate milk or hot chocolate?" she asks.

I look out the window to evaluate. We have

3

chocolate milk when it's hot out and cocoa when it's cold. It's early September, so we're almost getting into cocoa weather. The late afternoon sun makes warm gold rectangles on our walls, and it's starting to smell like fall in the park. But I'm not ready for winter yet.

"Milk chocolate want I," I say, talking backward without realizing it. My hero is the brilliant and talented Leonardo da Vinci. He wrote backward sometimes, so I decided talking backward was a good idea, too. Only my friends can understand me when I do it. It's good when we need to talk secretly and grown-ups are listening.

Mom, however, has declared our house a No Backward Talk zone. She says if I talk backward to her, she'll answer me in Latin, and we'll never get anywhere.

I realize she's giving me the you-just-talked-backward-to-me look. "I mean, I want chocolate milk," I add quickly.

She smiles. "You got it." She pulls herself up and heads for the kitchen, which is about the size of a broom closet. Mom has a job at the library, but we still don't have very much money. She spends one day a week tutoring women who can't read, and she doesn't get paid for that at all. Mom is really smart, and if she'd wanted to, I know she could have been a banker like her sister, my aunt Thelma. But Mom told me she and Thelma have different priorities. Which I think means that Aunt Thelma wanted to get rich and Mom didn't.

I don't care about the money most of the time. I don't need fancy clothes or MP3 players or video games. But there's one thing I really, *really* want: a computer. When I go over to see my friends the triplets, they let me use theirs.

Once, when we were all hanging out in Jerzey Mae's room, I found a Web site that lists all sorts of fascinating diseases. Unfortunately, I made the mistake of reading the symptoms of beriberi aloud. Jerzey Mae got paler and paler as I read.

"*My* muscles ache," she said. "*I'm* tired." She sank back into a pile of puffy pink pillows.

"Are you irritable?" I asked.

"Yes, she is," her sister JoAnn answered for her. Jerzey Mae smacked JoAnn with one of the pillows. "See?" said JoAnn.

"Do you have appetite loss?" I continued.

"Yes!" Jerzey said.

Jessica, her other sister, pointed out that we *had* just eaten huge hot-fudge sundaes. But Jerzey got so freaked out that she tried to convince her parents to take her to the emergency room. Her mom said we couldn't look at that Web site anymore.

I go into the kitchen and start measuring out chocolate powder for my drink. I dip the scoop into the container, then level it off carefully with a knife till it's exactly even.

Out of the corner of my eye I see Mom grinning at me.

"You'll be glad I'm precise when I'm a doctor and you're coming to me for a prescription," I say.

"You got that right," she replies.

I've wanted to be a doctor ever since I read about Leonardo cutting up dead bodies so he could see how they worked. I figured that whatever's in a body must be really interesting if it's enough to make someone want to do that. And, as always, Leonardo was right. There's so much going on in a human body it's amazing we can even stand up.

Mom drops the pasta into a pot of boiling water. Then she slathers French bread with garlic butter and pops it under the broiler.

"Can we play Scrabble after dinner?" I ask.

"Yup," she says. "And I'll kick your butt this time." She starts to do an extremely premature victory dance, waving a kitchen towel around as she sashays in a circle.

"Will not," I say. I see the tickle-glint in Mom's eye and start to back out of the room.

"Will too!" she says, lunging for my especially ticklish right side.

I shriek. "No . . . fair!" I gasp, laughing. She knows exactly where to tickle me, but apparently *she* was born tickle-proof. My anatomy books do not show diagrams of tickle zones.

The phone rings. "Keep an eye on the garlic bread," she says as she runs into the living room.

"Hello? . . . Oh, hello, Thelma," she says.

That's a little weird. My mom and her sister get along okay, but they don't talk much, even though Thelma lives only an hour away. In a very big house in a very fancy suburb, ever since she married a very rich lawyer, on top of having all her own rich-banker money.

". . . Oh, dear, I'm sorry to hear that. Yes, of course we can help . . . Tuesday? Yes, that will be fine. That's my day off, so I'll be here all afternoon . . . yes, we'll see her then. Good-bye."

Oh, no. Please let "her" be anyone— *anyone*—other than my cousin Tiffany.

A burning smell wafts through the air. I grab an oven mitt and yank the very-toasted garlic bread out of the oven as Mom returns. She has an odd look on her face.

"Well," she says.

I brace myself for bad news.

"Your aunt and uncle are going out of town. And the nanny who takes care of your cousin Tiffany is leaving town, too. The nanny's mother is having surgery on her knee."

I perk up. "Can I watch?" I've always wanted to see an operation. I'm not grossed out by blood or intestines or anything. The only thing that makes me squeamish is when JoAnn turns her eyelids inside out, and I doubt a doctor would turn her eyelids inside out during knee surgery.

Mom stares at me. "Of course you can't watch, Dr. Smarty-Pants," she replies. "The point *is*, all the adults will be gone, so Tiffany is coming to stay with us for a while."

No wonder my scalp is tingling. "A *while*? How long is a while?"

"A week or two, more or less."

I'm hoping for less. Much less. My cousin Tiffany wears designer clothes. Her house looks like one of those rock-star houses you see on TV. When Mom dragged me to Tiffany's tenth birthday party, Tiffany talked nonstop about every one of her new outfits and all of her jewelry and her brand-new flat-screen TV and her video games. When one of her friends asked me if I had a PlayStation, Tiffany laughed and said, "No, she just has a lot of books," before I could even open my mouth. And when she visited our apartment last year, I left the room for a minute and came back to find her sprinkling blue powder onto a crown she was making for her stupid dog.

"That's the copper sulfate from my chemistry set!" I yelled.

"It's a pretty color, isn't it?" she said, holding up the crown to admire it.

That was the last straw. I bet real scientists don't have to worry about people stealing their chemicals to decorate dog hats.

Mom tosses the pasta, cuts the garlic bread in diagonal slices the way I like, and carries everything to the table. I usually love our cozy apartment, but now I can't help looking at it through Tiffany's eyes. It wasn't decorated by New York's top interior designer, the way her house was. There are no expensive glass art pieces on the tables or oil paintings on the walls. I look down at our dishes—they're all mismatched, because Mom thinks that's cool. I usually like them, too, but I bet Tiffany will think we can't afford matching dishes.

I take a bite of garlic bread, but it doesn't taste as good as usual. "Does she have to?" I finally say.

Mom looks at me sympathetically. "Look, I know you two don't have much in common. Her mom and I don't, either. But maybe you'll find things to appreciate about each other if you spend more time together."

I, for one, seriously doubt it.

Chapter 2

"Maybe it won't be that bad," Jessica says.

We're walking up the stairs to the Nutcracker School of Ballet for our first class of the fall season. Jessica's sisters, JoAnn and Jerzey Mae, are on the stairs ahead of us. I stay behind with Jessica, who walks a little slower because one of her legs is shorter than the other. I once told her that no one has a body that's exactly the same on both sides— everyone has one foot that's bigger than the other or an arm that's a little longer. That made her feel better. Which is good, because talking to *her* always makes *me* feel better. I can tell her I'm dreading Tiffany's visit, and I know Jessica won't tell me I'm a horrible, awful person for wishing my cousin would get beamed up by aliens.

"What won't be that bad?" Epatha asks, out of breath from racing up the stairs. She pulls her long, wavy hair back into a bun as we step inside and head to the waiting room.

"Brenda's cousin Tiffany is coming to stay with her for a while," Jessica tells her.

"*That* cousin?" Epatha stares at me in horror. "Little Miss Snooty Girl, who brags about everything?" Last year, when Tiffany was visiting, we went to Bella Italia, the restaurant Epatha's family owns. Tiffany said it was "quaint" to eat in a restaurant without tablecloths. She talked about all the fancy places where she's eaten, turned up her nose at Bella Italia's amazing tortellini, then pointed out a microscopic chip in the bottom of her dinner plate. (Who looks *underneath* a dinner plate?) Epatha would have poured a pitcher of orange soda down Tiffany's back if her mom

14

hadn't yanked her away just in time.

Jessica gives Epatha a meaningful look. "I was just telling Brenda that maybe it won't be so bad."

"You *loca*, crazy girl?" Epatha says. Her mom is from Puerto Rico, and her dad is from Italy, so she speaks Spanish, Italian, and English—often all at once. "Of course it's going to be bad." She puts her arm around me. "You just gotta have a plan. Bring her back to the restaurant so Fabio can spill red sauce all over her fancy clothes. Reprogram her iPod so it only plays elevator music. Borrow Jessica's iguana and put him in your cousin's bed."

Now it's Jessica's turn to look horrified. Her animals are her best friends, next to all of us. I still think it's worth a shot.

I give Jessica my best of-course-you-can-trust-me-with-your-lizard smile. "Could I borrow Herman just for one—"

15

"Absolutely not," she says. She looks hurt that I'd even dream of asking, and I feel bad.

"I'm sorry. I just really don't want Tiffany to stay with us." I sigh.

We sit down on a bench and pull on our ballet slippers. "Okay," I continue. "I am going to be logical about this. I'm sure she doesn't want to stay with us any more than I want to have her there. There is no reason to waste my time getting annoyed." Still, I flop over on the bench like my backbone has just dissolved.

"That's right," Jessica says soothingly. "I'm sure Leonardo da Vinci had to put up with difficult people, too."

I have to say that Jessica was very clever to bring up Leonardo. Just the sound of his name calms me down and inspires me to act in an intelligent way.

"Hi, guys." Al comes in and sits on the floor beside our bench.

"Where's your tutu?" Epatha asks.

Al tosses a ballet shoe at Epatha and grins. Al just moved to Harlem from Georgia a few months ago. Her mom's a fancy clothing designer. She made Al wear a huge, glittery tutu and tights with pink lightning bolts on the rear end to her first ballet class. I wasn't there, but I've heard the story many times. But then her mom came to her senses. Now Al gets to wear normal clothes, like the brown leotard and brown tights she's wearing today.

Terrel marches into the room. "Hi," she says. She sits down and pulls her shoes off. Her movements are smooth and exact. No wasted effort. Leonardo would have admired her efficiency.

"The Sugar Plum Sisters, together again at last," Epatha says, grinning at us. We've been the Sugar Plum Sisters since this past summer, when Epatha, Terrel, Jerzey, JoAnn, Jessica, and I helped Al perform her dance for our summer show.

"At last? It's only been two weeks since the end of the summer session," Terrel says.

Epatha hugs Terrel, mostly to annoy her, since Terrel is not the huggy type. "But I've missed you so much, *mia cara!*" She pretends to plant kisses all over Terrel's head, till Terrel squirms away.

A girl wearing a sparkling tiara comes over. "Excuse me," she says to Terrel. "The teensy-weensy-little-baby class is upstairs." She puts her hands on her hips and smirks.

Tiara Girl has been in my class forever, unfortunately. She knows very well that Terrel is in our class, too. Terrel is a year younger than us, but she's an excellent dancer. Tiara Girl just likes to stir things up. Having that heavy tiara on her head probably affects the circulation of blood to her brain.

"Excuse me," Terrel says with exaggerated politeness. "The warthog class is in Africa, so you'd better get on a plane."

19

In our last show, Tiara Girl had to dance in a warthog costume. You can tell she's not happy to be reminded of this. But just as she's about to say something else, Ms. Debbé comes into the room. She's wearing a turban, as always, and dramatic makeup, as always. A carved wooden box nestles in the curve of her right arm. She taps her walking stick on the floor for attention.

"The class, it begins. Follow me, ladies," she says, in a thick French accent. She turns and heads up the stairs.

We clomp up the stairs behind her.

"So does that box mean we get the Shoe Talk today?" Al asks.

"You bet we do," Epatha says. "Nap time, Sugar Plum Sisters."

"Hey," Al pokes her. "I *want* to hear it again. It's interesting."

"That's 'cause you've only heard it once before," Epatha says. "We've all heard it *mil veces*, a million times."

"Nine times," I correct her.

"Whatever," Epatha says. "I could give that talk in my sleep."

We go through the door on the left, at the top of the stairs, into Studio 1, my favorite classroom. High windows line the left side of the room. Sunlight pools on the honey-colored wood floor.

"Please sit," Ms. Debbé says.

We sit on the floor. I look around. I don't see any new kids, just the same people who took the class in the summer. The triplets sit right behind us. JoAnn is still wearing her baseball cap, which Ms. Debbé will ask her to take off right about . . .

"JoAnn, please remove your cap," Ms. Debbé says.

JoAnn hastily reaches up and pulls it off.

"Now. Welcome to the fall session of the Nutcracker School of Ballet. I know you all.

21

You all know me. We all know how important the dance—the movement—is. But I think there is one other thing we should be reminded of."

She opens the wooden box, lifts out a piece of yellowed tissue paper, and removes a pair of very old-looking toeshoes. "You all know that these are my most prized possessions. They are the toeshoes of Miss Camilla Freeman, the very first black prima ballerina with the Ballet Company of New York. She did something that many thought was not possible. By working hard, she opened doors for other black dancers all over the world."

She holds up the shoes so we can see them. The sole of the right shoe has Miss Camilla Freeman's autograph scrawled in black pen.

"So, why do I show you these shoes? Why?" Ms. Debbé continues.

"Yeah, why?" Epatha whispers. "Why, why, *why*?"

Al shoves her.

"For one, she was my teacher. When I came to this country, she taught me very well. When we both lived in the ballet school dormitory, she took care of me, since I was so far from home. By looking at these shoes again, I remind myself of her good teaching so I can teach you better. But mostly, these shoes represent . . ."

"Potential," JoAnn says under her breath.

"Potential," Epatha says, rolling her eyes.

"Potential," Ms. Debbé says. "These shoes prove that nothing is impossible. If you have a dream, you can achieve it."

She lovingly wraps the tissue around the shoes and places them back in the box as gently as if they were eggs. Then she closes the lid and puts the box on a table by the door.

"Now. To the barre," she says.

After class ends, we go back downstairs to put our street shoes on.

"Shoot," says Terrel. "I forgot to tell Ms. Debbé I'm going to miss class on Saturday." She races up the stairs to Ms. Debbé's office.

"Why's she missing class?" I ask Jessica.

"One of her brothers is in a martial arts demonstration," Jessica says. "He said that since he had to go to our last dance show, she'd better show up for his karate thing or he'd karate-chop her."

"I'd like to see him try it," Al snorts. Even though Terrel is tiny, she's the last person I'd mess with. If her brother tried to karate-chop her, he'd end up with a broken patella (that means "kneecap").

We walk outside, where a bunch of grown-ups wait for us. Jessica squeezes my arm. "Good luck," she says. "I hope Tiffany's not too bad."

It had been so much fun being back in class with my friends that I'd almost forgotten about Tiffany. "Thanks," I say. Appropriately, a cloud picks this moment to drift in front of the sun. The temperature drops instantly, and I shiver.

One of Epatha's big sisters comes over to us. She's going to walk me home, since Mom has to wait at the apartment for Tiffany to show up. "You ready?" she asks.

Epatha sees me hesitate. "Oh, come on," she says. "We have five whole blocks to think of horrible things we can do to Miss Moneybags."

I know I can't actually do anything horrible to Tiffany. But the idea cheers me up anyway. I adjust my backpack and take a deep breath. "Let's go," I say.

Chapter 3

I use my key to open the door of our building. Maybe Tiffany won't be here yet. But when I approach our apartment, that hope is shattered by a series of piercing yaps.

Pookiepie.

Sure enough, when I open the door, a tiny dog lunges at me. The pink bow on his head bobs from side to side as he bares his tiny teeth, growls, and tries to nip my ankles. A pile of shiny red luggage sits in our hallway.

"Pookiepie!" Tiffany comes into the hall and scoops up the fur ball. "Hi," she says, glancing at me.

"Hi," I reply.

Tiffany holds Pookiepie up to her face and

coos. I'm pretty tall for my age, but she's even taller. Her long hair is braided into cornrows studded with little beads. I can tell that her jeans, which are covered with sparkly rhinestone swirls, cost more than all my clothes put together.

Mom appears in the doorway. "Hi, honey," she says, kissing me. "Tiffany just got here."

"Oh," I say.

"Why don't you help her unpack while I get to work on dinner?"

Tiffany and I carry her bags into my room. Actually, *I* carry the bags—Tiffany won't put Pookiepie down, so she only manages to bring in a small overnight case.

"Where am I going to sleep?" she says, looking around my tiny bedroom.

27

"You can have the bed," I say. "I'll sleep on an air mattress on the floor." I am not happy about this arrangement, but yesterday Mom gave me a lecture about being nice to guests. I'd countered with the very logical point that giving Tiffany my bed would involve doing more laundry, since we'd have to wash my sheets twice. However, she says good manners are more important than logic. I love my mother, but she does not have a scientific mind.

Tiffany sits on my bed and looks around. Not that there's much to see: my bookshelf, the desk where I do my homework, my alarm clock.

She bounces experimentally on my bed. As she does, the rhinestones on her jeans catch the light and make colored spots that jump up and down on my wall. "My bed is softer than this," she remarks. "And it's king size."

What am I supposed to say? "I guess you

need one so you can sleep with your enormous dog."

The irony is lost on her. "Oh, no. Pookiepie has his own bed. Mom got it at a specialty pet shop. It's made of velvet, and it cost three hundred and fifty dollars. It has little pillows with rhinestones on them. Doesn't it, Honeybunny?" She rubs her nose against Pookiepie's.

Are all rich people crazy? No, the triplets' parents have a lot of money. Their house is nice, but Herman sleeps in a cage, not a three-hundred-and-fifty-dollar iguana bed.

"Who's that weird old guy on the wall?" Tiffany asks.

Blood rushes to my face. "That is not a weird old guy," I say as calmly as I can. "That is Leonardo da Vinci."

"Pfff," she says. "Looks like a weird old guy to me." She turns away, fishes around in her suitcase, and pulls out a tiny little dog treat for Pookiepie.

Weird old guy? The most brilliant thinker and artist in the last thousand years? I have the illogical urge to hit Tiffany over the head with my most prized possession, a book of Leonardo's paintings and drawings. It is a very large, very heavy book. Instead, I take a few deep breaths. According to my medical books, deep breaths are supposed to bring more oxygen to your cells and calm you down. It doesn't work.

"Dinner!" my mom calls.

Thank goodness.

We join her at the table. She's made hamburgers for Tiffany and herself and a veggie burger for me.

"Why do you have different food?" Tiffany asks me.

"Oh, Brenda's been a vegetarian since she found out Leonardo was one," Mom says.

"Leonardo DiCaprio?" Tiffany asks.

"Leonardo da Vinci," I say between gritted

teeth. "The weird old guy."

Mom steers the conversation in a different direction. "So, Tiffany, what have you been up to? Are your parents still really busy at work?" We haven't seen Tiffany since her birthday party three months ago. Three months is way too long when you're waiting for Christmas, and way too short when you're talking about time between Tiffany encounters. I think Einstein's theory of relativity says something about this, but I don't really know for sure yet. I've planned out all my science studies for the next eight years, and physics isn't till seventh grade.

Tiffany swallows a mouthful of food. "Dad's still gone a lot, and Mom works all the time." She's quiet for a minute. Then she perks up. "You know what? We just got our swimming pool redone. There's a fountain at the end and everything, and little blue rocks all over the bottom of the pool. I go swimming

31

a lot. I like riding horses, too. Do you have horses?"

Mom and I exchange a look. "New York City is not exactly the best place to keep horses," Mom says.

"Oh, I forgot," Tiffany replies.

Horses or no horses, I am not one bit jealous of Tiffany's house in the suburbs. In the city we have museums all over the place. What kind of educational opportunities do you have in the suburbs? The only thing I like about her house is the creek that runs beside it. I'll bet there's a lot of interesting bacteria in there. I'd like to analyze them, but since I don't have a microscope yet, even that doesn't matter.

Mom asks Tiffany how often she goes riding.

"Twice a week," she says. "Sometimes I ride Champion. He's black and white. But sometimes I ride King Hal. He's a palomino.

Wait—I have a picture of me riding him on my computer, so I can show you. My lessons cost a hundred dollars an hour. Mom says riding will make me more poised. Besides, one of my friends moved to England, and rich people there play polo. You know what polo is? They play it on horses. Anyway, someday I might go visit my friend, so I need to know about horses, so I can watch the polo matches better."

Mom looks like she's sorry she asked.

"I'll help with the dishes," I say quickly when dinner's over.

"That's okay. Why don't you two go hang out while I clean up?" She gives me a look that says, "Just *try* to get along with her."

I give her a look that says, "Do I *have* to?"

She gives me a look that says, "Yes, you *have* to."

So I slowly follow Tiffany down the hall back to my room.

"Want to see my clothes?" Tiffany asks.

"Sure," I lie.

Instead of opening her suitcases, she burrows under them for a briefcaselike bag, opens it, and pulls out . . . of course: a fancy laptop, exactly the kind I would get if I had a million dollars.

She presses a button, and the computer comes to life. A row of pictures appears on the screen. I can't believe it—she's actually taken pictures of all her clothes.

"Look, look—this is the dress Mom got me in Paris when she was there on business. And . . ."

I pretend to look at the screen, but I'm not listening. I am so jealous I can hardly breathe. I don't care if she has all the stupid clothes in the world, but a computer . . . I could do a lot with a computer.

". . . And look at this one—it's designer! I wore it to the ballet. It was a special tribute to Miss Camilla Freeman. *You've* probably never

heard of her, but she's very famous. She was the very first black dancer to dance with the Ballet Company of New York." She gives me a smug smile.

"I *know* who Miss Camilla Freeman is," I hear myself saying. "I have a pair of her toeshoes. Autographed."

What just came out of my mouth? It's as if an alien just took over my body. I wait to see what the alien will say next.

"You do?" she asks.

My mind is racing—but not as fast as my alien-controlled mouth. "Yes."

She looks at me suspiciously. "Where are they?"

"I lent them to a friend. She wanted to show her mom." Why don't I say I was just kidding? Now I know what Mom means when she talks about digging yourself deeper into a hole.

Tiffany squints at me. "I don't believe you. I want to see them."

"Oh, I'll get them back when I see my friend," I say airily. "But it won't be till my ballet class on Saturday. You might be gone by then," I add, crossing my fingers and hoping her nanny's mom recovers fast.

"Nope. I'll definitely be here for at least two weeks," Tiffany replies.

"Great," I say. "Then I guess you'll get to see them."

*   *   *

I lie awake for a very long time that night. I can hear Tiffany's even breathing and Pookiepie's snuffly snores coming from my bed. I keep sliding around on the air mattress, but that's not what's keeping me up.

How could I have told Tiffany I had Miss Camilla Freeman's toeshoes?

In one of my medical books, it says that your body releases something called adrenaline when you're under stress. It can make you stronger or faster than normal, so you can lift up a car if an old lady's trapped under it or run from a bear. The book doesn't mention that it can make you tell ridiculous lies to your cousin, but maybe that's what just happened.

Regardless, Leonardo definitely would not have approved.

Chapter 4

The next morning I wake up with a knot in my stomach. It takes me a minute to remember what's wrong. When I do, I groan and roll over. I wonder if Tiffany will just forget about the shoes.

The tick-tick-tick of dog claws echoes in the hallway. The door opens and Pookiepie bursts through. He heads right for my sneakers, which are lying by my bed, and starts gnawing on the toe of the left one. I yank the now-slobbery shoe from his mouth as Mom pops her head in my door.

"You awake? We just took Pookiepie for a walk. Hurry up—we need to get going."

I get dressed and splash some water on my

face. Tiffany's sitting at the table, staring at the cereal box like it's from Mars.

"Our cook always makes me bacon, toast, and an omelet," she says. Today she's wearing a T-shirt with a designer's name plastered across the front, another pair of fancy jeans, and a beret. Who puts on a hat to go to breakfast?

"Well, cereal will be a nice change for you, then," Mom replies. Her voice is a little higher-pitched than usual.

I pour myself a bowl of cornflakes. "Is Tiffany coming to school with me?" I ask, trying not to sound horrified.

"No," Mom says. "She brought her own schoolwork with her. She'll go to Mrs. Appleton's while I'm gone." Mrs. Appleton is the nice old lady down the hall. Last week she gave me the tiny human skeleton model her son used when he was in medical school. She definitely doesn't deserve to spend the day with Tiffany.

"I'd never go to a public school," Tiffany

says. "I only go to private schools. Mom told me about the public school you went to when you were little. She said the environment was not conducive to learning." She turns to me. "*Conducive* means . . ."

"Brenda *knows* what conducive means," Mom says. I can see her rolling her eyes as she leaves the room.

Mom's right. It means "tending to cause or bring about." The way Tiffany acts is *conducive* to my smacking her on the head.

But I've got more important things to think about: those stupid ballet slippers. If I'm going to confess, I'd better get it over with. "Tiffany, about Miss Camilla Freeman's shoes . . ." I say quickly, before Mom comes back.

"Yes, I'm really looking forward to seeing them," she says, neatly dabbing at her mouth with her napkin. "How did you get them?"

"Well, that's the thing . . ." I begin.

She interrupts. "I have to say, I'm surprised.

Those toeshoes are a real piece of history. They must be worth a lot of money. I never thought that *you* would have anything *I'd* be jealous of." She doesn't say this in a mean way; it's more a matter-of-fact, just-stating-the-obvious way, which shows you how clueless she is.

But I get mad anyway. My confession evaporates on my tongue. "Well, I guess you were wrong, weren't you?"

"Five minutes," Mom calls.

"Aren't you supposed to put milk on cereal?" Tiffany asks. I'm so distracted that I forgot. No wonder my mouth feels like it's full of sawdust.

Mom comes back in. "Brenda, Al's mom will drop you off at Epatha's after school, and I'll pick you up at five. Okay?"

I give her a grateful smile. She could have asked Al's mom to drop me off at Mrs. Appleton's after school. She winks at me.

*　　*　　*

It's only the second day of school. On the first day, our new teacher, Mr. Tork, arranged our desks in a big circle around the room. He said we could sit anywhere we wanted to, "unless we abuse the privilege." It took Kevin Phelan exactly two minutes to abuse the privilege by putting a chicken sandwich on Chloe Tucker's chair right before she sat down. Now Kevin sits next to Mr. Tork.

I get to school a little early, so I'm already at my desk when Al arrives. "What's wrong with you?" she asks, sitting down beside me.

I hesitate for a minute. I hate it when I do stupid things, and I really hate it when other people find out about them. But Al's my friend. I know she felt stupid last summer when she had so much trouble learning the Sugar Plum Fairy's dance. So, I tell her about lying to Tiffany.

"Wow," she says. "What are you going to do?"

I shake my head. "Got any ideas?"

She smiles. "No. But I know someone who might."

Terrel's classroom is three doors down from ours. At recess, we catch Terrel in the hallway. Al tells her the problem. Terrel runs her tongue along her crooked teeth and scrunches her eyes up, the way she always does when she's thinking. She doesn't bother telling me how stupid I've been, which I already know; she just gets to work figuring out how to fix the problem. This is why I love Terrel.

"Sugar Plum emergency meeting," she says. "At Epatha's. I'll tell the triplets." Terrel managed to talk her dad into getting her a cell phone, since she has to organize things for all her older brothers. Even though she's the youngest, she keeps their house running like a finely tuned machine. She decides which brother buys the family groceries, which one picks her up from school, and which one gets her dad's dry cleaning. They've stopped complaining, because if they follow her orders, everything gets done right. She is a natural-born leader.

The triplets go to a different school than we do. So does Epatha, but since she knows I'm coming over to her restaurant after school, she'll be there anyway.

"Thanks, Terrel," I say.

She turns neatly and marches down the hall.

It's four o'clock. Jessica, Jerzey Mae, JoAnn, Al, Terrel, and I are all sitting in a bright red vinyl booth at the back of Bella Italia. There aren't many customers at this time of day, but we can still hear clattering coming from the kitchen. The wonderful smell of fresh garlic bread fills the air.

Epatha comes over balancing a tray of soft drinks. Most are a weird brown color, because she likes to mix orange, cola, lemon-lime, and root beer together into a drink she calls the Bella Bombshell. It tastes surprisingly good. She hands a glass of plain lemon-lime soda to Jerzey, who is a bit squeamish, then doles the rest out and sits down with us. "Okay, so what's going on?" she asks.

45

I clear my throat. "I told my cousin Tiffany I had Miss Camilla Freeman's toeshoes," I say, "and that I would show them to her on Saturday."

"What's the big deal?" JoAnn asks. "Go buy some toeshoes and drag them around in the dirt so they look old."

I can hear Epatha's mom clearing off the table behind me, so I switch to the backward talk that grown-ups can't understand. "Tell could she," I say. "Then did they than now different look toeshoes." Epatha's mom moves away. "I read a book about them once," I say switching back to normal talk.

"Of course you did," JoAnn says. She doesn't get the whole reading thing. She wants to be a professional skateboarder and says she doesn't need to read. I once pointed out to JoAnn that she'd still need to read the contracts for all her product-endorsement deals, but she said she'd make her uncle the lawyer do it.

Jessica looks at me. "Why did you tell Tiffany the shoes were yours?"

I flush. "I don't know. She was just talking about all this stuff she has, and then she pulled out a computer. . . ." My voice trails off. It sounds like a pretty lame excuse now, and it's hard to explain how mad I felt at the time.

But Jessica nods like she understands. "Maybe you should just tell her the truth."

"Of *course* she shouldn't tell her the truth!" Epatha roars. She slams her hands down on the table, making the silverware rattle. I get the feeling she's been waiting for this moment ever since last year, when she didn't get to pour the orange soda down Tiffany's back. "You need to put Little Miss Rich Girl in her place. All she cares about is stuff, so *you* need to have something better than what *she's* got. We just need to get those toeshoes from Ms. Debbé."

Jerzey Mae looks at her, eyes wide with

alarm. "You mean *steal* them?" she says.

"We aren't going to *steal* them," Epatha says. "We'll just borrow them."

We all automatically look at Terrel, who has been quiet this whole time. Since she's the most practical thinker, I expect her to shoot down Epatha's idea immediately. But she surprises me.

"Right," Terrel says. "We take the shoes Saturday after class. The school's closed Sunday and Monday. Tuesday we sneak them back in. Ms. Debbé will never find out."

"We don't even know where she keeps the shoes," I say weakly. "Maybe Jessica's right. Maybe I should just tell Tiffany I lied."

"*I* know where she keeps them," Terrel says, dropping her voice.

We all lean in.

"Where?" asks JoAnn.

"I was in her office after class last week while she was putting them away," says Terrel.

"They're in her bottom-right desk drawer." She slurps the last bit of soda out of her glass, then licks the end of her straw. "And she probably only takes them out at the beginning of each session. I doubt she pulls them out to talk to them every day. We can get them, easy."

I'm not so sure. This plan is starting to feel like a flu epidemic I read about—it didn't seem bad at first, but it grew and grew, and all of a sudden people were keeling over everywhere.

"Well? What do you think?" Terrel asks.

I look around the table. Everyone looks as if they think this is a good plan—everyone but Jerzey Mae and Jessica. Jerzey Mae's scared of everything, so it's easy to ignore her reluctance. But Jessica is looking at me with disappointed eyes, as if I should be bigger than this. I look away quickly.

"Okay," I say. "Let's do it."

Chapter 5

As always, Terrel comes up with the plan. Ms. Debbé's office is on the third floor of the Nutcracker School. Ms. Debbé's son, Mr. Lester, teaches at the school too, and he's usually around during our classes. But he's going out of town this weekend, so he won't be here to catch us up on the third floor, where we're not supposed to be.

On Saturday after class, Epatha will stay behind in the classroom and ask Ms. Debbé for help with a routine we're just learning.

Al will hang around outside the studio and whistle if she sees Ms. Debbé coming.

Terrel and I will sneak into Ms. Debbé's office and get the shoes.

JoAnn will go outside the school and tell all the grown-ups waiting to pick us up that we had to go to the bathroom.

Jerzey Mae will not do anything, because she is a terrible liar. Jessica will not do anything, because she is morally opposed to the plan. I am secretly glad that I am not making criminals out of *all* of my friends.

But it sounds like Terrel's got everything figured out. She even has a plan to get the shoes back into Ms. Debbé's office, but she won't tell us what it is yet.

"Focus on one thing at a time," Terrel says on Saturday as we climb up the steps to the school together. "You all just worry about your jobs today."

I'm a little nervous but also relieved that soon I can show the shoes to Tiffany, and that this will all be over in seventy-two hours. Not that I'm counting.

Our troubles start when Mr. Lester greets us at the front door. "Hello, ladies," he says, holding the door open for us. He's neatly dressed as always, in a dark brown sweater, the same color as his tidy beard and mustache.

"He's supposed to be out of town!" Epatha hisses at Terrel.

"I thought you were going away for the weekend," Al says to Mr. Lester.

"Trying to get rid of me?" He grins at us.

Epatha steps on my toe hard. "Ow!" I say. Terrel shoots us a dirty look.

Mr. Lester shuffles the papers he's carrying. "We're having some people come paint the school tomorrow and Monday," he says. "So I decided I'd better hang around." He goes upstairs.

JoAnn turns to Terrel. "What do we do now?" she asks as we head into the waiting room.

Terrel takes off her street shoes and puts

them under the bench. She lines up the toes and the heels and fusses with them until they are exactly even. I know under all that fussing she's thinking up a storm. Other girls drift into the room and start warming up.

"Stick to the plan," Terrel finally says. "We just have to be ready to call it off if he's in the way."

We start our class at the barre, the same as always. As we plié up and down, my stomach does pliés, too. I wonder if my friends are as nervous as I am. Epatha's going down lower and bouncing up higher than anyone. JoAnn looks bored, but she does all the moves well. Jerzey Mae keeps losing her balance and grabbing the barre for support, but that's normal. Terrel dips up and down neatly and efficiently. Al had to work hard to catch up with our class, but she looks good now, and even tosses in an extra arm flourish now and then, the way Epatha does. Jessica

moves in a graceful, dreamy way.

It must be the longest ballet class in the history of the planet. I keep checking the clock, thinking an hour must have gone by, and it turns out to be just a minute or two.

After our barre work, we do châiné turns across the room. It feels good to let go of some of my nervous energy. "Your turns, they are very good today, Brenda," Ms. Debbé says in her thick French accent. She gives me an encouraging pat as I reach the end of the

room. This makes me feel even worse about "borrowing" her shoes.

But just as I decide we need to call everything off, the clock speeds up. I try to catch Terrel's attention, but I can't. Ms. Debbé ends the class. The triplets race off to stall our parents. As Terrel pulls me out the door, I hear Epatha asking Ms. Debbé about a combination we learned last week. "I really don't get it. Can you show me slowly? Really, *really* slowly?"

Al follows us and takes her position at the bottom of the stairway. Terrel and I continue up. My legs feel like they weigh a hundred pounds each, and it's not from all the pliés we just did. "Let's just forget it," I say.

"Shhh . . . Mr. Lester!" Terrel says. He's standing in the big classroom on the third floor with a guy in white overalls. They're holding some paint chips up against the wall and talking. We creep down the other side of the hallway and hope he doesn't see us.

A toilet flushes, and a little Ballet One girl comes out of the bathroom. She's wearing a pink T-shirt and tights, like all the Ballet One girls. They used to wear leotards and tights. But that's a lot of clothes for a little kid to take off every time she goes to the bathroom, and most of them didn't make it in time. After a few accidents, Ms. Debbé said T-shirts were perfectly acceptable ballet wear.

The girl stares at us with big eyes as we

pass her. "Is everyone in the world up here today?" I whisper.

"*Shhhh!*" Terrel says.

Ms. Debbé's door is slightly open. We're just a few steps away when we hear an obnoxious voice behind us.

"What are you girls doing up here?" Tiara Girl asks. She puts her hands on her hips as if she were a teacher in the school yard at lunch.

Terrel and I look at each other. The sound of the toilet being flushed must have drowned out Al's whistled warning.

"What are *you* doing here?" Terrel asks. My eyes dart over to the big classroom. Mr. Lester and the paint guy aren't paying any attention to us.

"Going to the bathroom. Not that it's any of your business," Tiara Girl replies. She reaches up and adjusts her tiara, probably just to make sure we notice that it's a new one with pink and purple rhinestones.

"So are we," says Terrel.

We're closer to the bathroom door than Tiara Girl. "Why don't you go ahead?" I say.

She looks at me suspiciously. "Why?"

We're wasting time. Who knows how long Mr. Lester will be focusing on those paint chips? So I say, "I feel sick after those pirouettes. I may have to throw up. It's going to smell pretty bad in there after I'm done."

Tiara Girl runs into the bathroom and slams the door.

"Quick!" says Terrel.

We duck into Ms. Debbé's office. It kind of looks like a ballet star's dressing room (which makes sense, since she was a ballet star when she was younger). A gold-framed mirror hangs on the wall, and a vase of lilies sits on a chest of drawers. A wooden desk sits in the middle of the room on a red Persian carpet. The smell of Ms. Debbé's fancy perfume hangs in the air.

"Bottom-right desk drawer," Terrel whispers.

I go around to the back of the desk. There are three drawers on the right side. I reach for the bottom one, but stop before I touch it.

"What about fingerprints?" I ask.

"What do you think this is, a TV show?" asks Terrel. "If she doesn't even know the shoes are gone, and we bring them right back, why would she look for fingerprints?"

I grab a tissue from the square pink box on Ms. Debbé's desk and use it to pull the drawer open, just in case.

The carved wooden box is right in front. I gingerly lift the lid. The shoes are inside, nestled in yellowed tissue paper. I carefully lift them out. I've seen them many times before, but touching them is different. These shoes actually danced across the stage of the Ballet Company of New York—with the feet of one of the world's most famous ballerinas inside them. Wow. It's almost as good as getting to touch a paintbrush Leonardo used.

Terrel pokes her head out the door of the office, then looks back at me. "Brenda, come on!" she hisses.

I return to the present. Then I realize our mistake. We've come straight from the studio, so we don't have our dance bags with us.

"What do I put them in?" I ask. "We can't just walk out with them."

We look around. Maybe there's a plastic bag we can take. But there isn't.

"We'll have to stick them down our leotards," Terrel says. "Give me one."

I hand her a shoe, and she shoves it into the neck-hole of her leotard. I do the same.

"Move it around to your side so your arm will hide it," Terrel tells me. I wiggle the shoe around until it's pointing up on my right side. "Let me see," she says. I turn toward her, trying to hold my right arm casually over the lump.

"Not too bad—we just need to move fast," she says. "How about me?"

"It looks like you have an enormous tumor on your rib," I say.

"A *what*?" she asks.

We hear the toilet flush again. "Run!" she says, pulling me out the door. We sprint down the stairs without looking back. Could Tiara Girl have seen us come out of Ms. Debbé's office?

We dash into the now-empty waiting room and pull the shoes out of our leotards. Terrel hands me hers and I put them in my bag. Then we put on our sneakers and jackets and run outside to where the grown-ups are waiting. Epatha, Al, and the triplets look at us, a question in their eyes. Terrel gives the thumbs-up. Epatha winks.

"Thanks, T.," I whisper before I head over

to Epatha and her sister, who are walking me home.

"Good luck," Terrel says.

But I won't need it. All I need to do is show Miss Camilla Freeman's shoes to Tiffany. In three days the shoes will be tucked away back where they belong, and I'll be off the hook. No more waking up in the middle of the night. It'll be as easy as reciting pi to the tenth digit, which I can do in my sleep.

Chapter 6

"I'm home!" I say, banging the front door behind me. My olfactory system alerts me to the presence of freshly baked chocolate-chip cookies (that means I smell them).

Mom comes out to greet me. She's wearing a green apron over her jeans, which she wipes her hands on before giving me a hug. "I'm making cookies for the library benefit," she says. "How was class?"

"Great," I say. "Where's Tiffany?" This may be the only time in my life I've ever wanted to see her. It would be too bad if we'd gone to all that trouble for nothing.

Mom heads back to the kitchen. "In your room. I think she's arranging all the pictures of her clothes by color. Or something. Want a cookie?"

"Not right now," I say. I head straight to my room.

Tiffany looks up from her computer as I come in. "Hi," she says. Pookiepie, who's curled at her feet, yaps and shows me his teeth, as if to remind me what a tough guy he is. But then he falls back asleep.

"Hi." I pull the door almost shut—shut enough so that Mom can't see us, but not so shut that she'll wonder what's going on. "I've got the shoes," I say softly.

Tiffany sits straight up. She pushes the computer aside. "Let's see," she says.

I unzip my bag. There they are, right on top. I slowly pull them out and put them on my bedspread.

Tiffany's mouth forms the word *oh*, but she doesn't say anything. I smile. For once I've actually shut her up.

She picks up the autographed shoe and holds it gently. "Wow," she finally says, running her fingers along the fabric. I look more closely, too. The shoe is made of light pink satin, with a leather sole. I haven't seen lots of toeshoes, but these definitely look different from the way toeshoes look today. The inside is yellowed with age, and the lining is peeling up from the bottom of the shoe. The shoe is signed in a perfect script, like something out of a penmanship book. There's a curlicue at the end of *Freeman*.

Tiffany looks at me. "You're acting like you've never seen them before," she says.

I shrug. "I just think they're cool, that's all," I reply.

"They sure are," she says, turning the other shoe around in her hand. "How did you get them?" she asks. Her tone of voice is different. It's like, before, she thought I was a couch or a table—something that just blended into the background, not really worth mentioning—but now I finally have her attention. It feels good.

"A friend got them for me," I say. This, at least, is not a total lie—Terrel did help me get them.

Mom's footsteps sound in the hall. I turn my body so my back is to the door and I'll be able to block her view of the shoes if she walks by my room.

"Hey, girls." She pops her head in the door. "If I spend one more minute in that kitchen, I'll go stark raving mad. Let's go get some pizza." She heads back down the hall.

Tiffany continues to inspect the shoes. I realize there's a very real danger she'll talk about them at lunch. Which would definitely interfere with my digestion. "Tiffany?" I say.

"What?" She lays the shoes carefully back on the bed.

"Um, don't mention the shoes to my mom, okay?"

"Why not?" she asks.

I am a facts person, not a fiction person. Making things up is not my strong point. "They were a present from one of her old boyfriends," I say. "He was Miss Camilla Freeman's son—a very famous choreographer. He . . . died in a tragic accident. Mom still gets very depressed when anything reminds her of him." I arrange my features to look as sad as possible.

Tiffany's eyes bug out. "That's terrible! How did he die?"

Well, I walked right into that one. "Um . . ." I look around the room for inspiration. I see the book *Treasure Island* on my shelf. "Pirates," I say.

"*Pirates?*"

"Well, not actual pirates. He was fishing on his boat. He thought he saw a pirate flag on a passing ship. He leaned out to get a better look, fell off the boat, and died."

"Couldn't he swim?" she asked. "I thought you had to be able to swim to get a boat license."

Rats—I forgot Tiffany's dad has a boat. "He had tetanus. That's a disease that makes your muscles freeze up. He couldn't move his legs, so he drifted into the boat's propeller and got chopped into a bunch of pieces." I apologize silently to Mom's fictional ex-boyfriend for the gruesome method of his demise, but surely this burst of gore will shut Tiffany up.

She looks at me, eyes wide with horror, but doesn't ask any more questions. I take advantage of her silence to tuck Miss Camilla Freeman's shoes under the comforter so Mom won't see them.

"Come on, girls," Mom calls. We grab our coats and follow her down the hall. Tiffany looks sick to her stomach. (More pizza for me!) I, however, feel as if I could soar through the air like one of the flying machines Leonardo designed.

We sit in one of the front booths at Bella Italia. Epatha's dad brings us a basket of garlic bread. He's a short, round man with a black mustache. "On the house," he says. He bows to Mom, giving us an extra-good look at the strip of hair combed over the top of his shiny, nearly bald head.

Epatha comes out from the kitchen and slides into the booth beside me. "Hi, Ms. Black," she says to Mom.

"Epatha, do you remember Brenda's cousin Tiffany?" Mom asks.

Epatha and Tiffany exchange unenthusiastic hellos. Tiffany looks Epatha up and down.

"I guess you can't wear nice clothes if you

work in a restaurant, right?" asks Tiffany.

Epatha looks just fine, in a normal T-shirt and jeans. I can see her start to turn red, and I'm wondering if this time she actually *will* pour orange soda down Tiffany's back. Fortunately, Epatha's mom senses that something is up and strides over. She's beautiful. She has glossy black hair and is wearing a green dress with lots of pink and orange flowers printed on it. She once told me the dress reminded her of the Puerto Rican rain forest near where she was born. She shoos Epatha back into the kitchen and takes our order. Before long we're diving into a deep-dish veggie special. Mom pours us root beers from the pitcher Epatha's mom brought us. We eat until we're stuffed.

We say good-bye to Epatha and her family, then slowly walk the five blocks back to our apartment. The sun warms the back of my neck. Kids roller-skate in the park, taking advantage of the nice, late-summer weather. I feel sleepy and happy. Mom unlocks the apartment door, and we go inside.

"I'm going to take a nap," I announce.

"Good idea," yawns Mom. She heads into her room.

I open the door to my room, with Tiffany close on my heels.

Pookiepie is on my bed, grunting and chewing. In his mouth is what's left of Miss Camilla Freeman's toeshoes.

Chapter 7

I stop dead in my tracks. I'm too stunned to even say anything. Tiffany pushes past me into the room, sees Pookiepie, and screams.

"What's going on?" Mom calls from her room.

"Nothing," Tiffany and I call back together.

Tiffany runs over and extracts the mass of fabric and ribbons from Pookiepie's mouth. The material is in shreds. The autographed part looks like Swiss cheese, with tooth holes all over it.

We both stare at the misshapen lumps in her hands. I'm not thinking much of anything. A tiny part of my brain understands that I'm in shock, which is your body's way of dealing with really bad situations. Like, if your finger gets chopped off, you may not feel any pain at first, because your body shuts down.

But at some point, the body starts working again. And, unfortunately, mine does that now. I sink down onto the floor. My heart is pounding so hard I can hear the blood rushing in my ears. What is Ms. Debbé going to say?

I almost forget that Tiffany's here until I hear a frightened voice behind my shoulder.

"You're not going to tell my mom, are you?"

I turn around. I've never seen Tiffany look scared before, but she sure does now. "I . . . I don't know," I say. I don't know what I'm going to do. I have $247.56 in my college fund—I wonder if that will get me someplace really far away, like Morocco or Uzbekistan.

"Please don't tell her," Tiffany begs. "She said that if Pookiepie ate any more shoes, she'd give him to the animal shelter. And if she finds out about *these* shoes . . ." A tear dribbles down the side of her nose.

For the second time in the last minute, I'm stunned. I've never seen Tiffany acting like a human being before. I thought she always got everything she wanted.

"Please don't tell anyone," Tiffany says again. "I'll give you my iPod. And my favorite video game. I'm *so* sorry about your shoes."

I look at her. I'm in so deep that keeping up the lie seems like more trouble than it's worth.

"They aren't my shoes," I say in a dull voice.

Tiffany looks puzzled. "Well, they *were* Miss Camilla Freeman's, but now they're yours, right?"

I shake my head. "They belong to my ballet teacher. I took them from her office earlier today. I was going to put them back. But now . . ."

I lie down on the floor with my hand over my eyes. I'm embarrassed that Leonardo is on my wall to see all this. I'm betting he never stole his ballet teacher's shoes.

Pookiepie comes over and sniffs my head. I open an eye and stare at him. Stupid dog, I think. It's all your fault.

But I know in my heart it isn't. I knew he was a shoe-chewer, but I left the shoes out anyway. Who's the stupid one?

Pookiepie inches closer to me. Then he licks my face with his smooth little tongue.

Tears burn the insides of my eyelids. I blink them away and sit up.

"I won't tell your mom," I say. "That's really awful, that she'd give your dog away."

Tiffany throws her arms around me. I'm too surprised to hug her back. "Thank you!" she says. "I won't tell yours, either. About— you know."

She nods at the shoes, which are lying in a forlorn heap on the bed.

I pick up the ex-left-shoe and turn it around in my hand. It doesn't matter whether Tiffany tells Mom or not. Someone's going to find out. Then what will happen to me?

Chapter 8

Tiffany and I stay in my room for the rest of the next day. Neither of us wants to face my mom, since moms can usually tell when you've done something wrong. They must have a special organ to sense it, but I've never seen it in any of my anatomy books.

When I go to the kitchen to get us some juice, Mom stops me. I brace myself. But all she says is, "You two are getting along better, aren't you?"

"Yeah." I try to smile, but it feels as if I'm wearing one of those mud masks ladies on TV shows stick on their faces. My cheeks barely move.

"I'm glad," she says, kissing the top of my head.

I wonder if they put kids in jail for stealing toeshoes. That would wreak havoc with my career plans.

The phone rings soon after I return to my room. Mom answers. "Just a second. I'll get her," Tiffany and I hear her say. Tiffany shoves the mangled toeshoes under the bed just as Mom sticks her head in the door. "Honey, it's Terrel," she says, handing me the phone.

"Thanks," I say. "Hello?" I try to sound normal, but my voice is higher than usual.

"Hey," says Terrel. "Did you show the shoes to Tiffany?"

"Uh . . . yes," I say.

"How did it go?"

"Not great," I answer, which may be the understatement of the century.

"Why? What happened?" Terrel asks.

"Um . . ." I hear Mom outside in the hallway, dusting off the bookshelves near my door, so I talk backward. "Snack little a had dog Tiffany's," I reply.

"What do I care what her stupid dog eats?" Terrel says.

I hear Mom moving farther down the hall. "Dogs chew on lots of things. Like *shoes*," I whisper.

There's silence on the end of the phone as Terrel tries to figure out what I'm talking about. Then she lets out an eardrum-piercing shriek. I pull the phone away from my head.

"That dumb dog *ate* Miss Camilla Freeman's shoes?" Terrel yells.

I keep my voice as calm as I can. "That is correct."

"Well, what are you going to do about it?" she hollers.

"Good question!" I say. "Do you have any suggestions?"

There is a dead silence on the other end of the line.

Apparently she does not have any suggestions. "Oh, man, oh, man, oh, man," she says. "We are in so much trouble."

"I am aware of that," I say. I collapse onto my bed. Tiffany's sitting on the floor staring into space, just like she's been doing for the last two hours. I've *never* seen her sitting on a floor before today.

Terrel exhales heavily into the phone. "Look, let me think about it. I'll call you back."

I hang up.

Tiffany looks at me.

"That was my friend Terrel. Sometimes

she's good at thinking up solutions to problems," I say.

Tiffany shakes her head. Her brown eyes look dull. "This one's hopeless," she says.

I hate to say it, but she may be right.

Chapter 9

Terrel doesn't call back. I find her in the hall at school on Monday morning.

"Sorry," she mumbles. "I can't think of anything. Not a single thing." She looks embarrassed. This is probably the first time ever she hasn't been able to think her way out of trouble.

My last bit of hope disappears like a puff of smoke. "That's okay," I tell her.

"Maybe she won't notice for a while," Terrel says. "Maybe we'll think of something."

I nod and turn down the hall toward my classroom. But I know it's just a matter of time.

*   *   *

On Tuesday I get to the Nutcracker School early. My skin is tingling like I have hives. My stomach churns like I have dysentery. My head aches like I have malaria. I wonder if I'll feel like this every single day until I'm found out.

There's a line for the first-floor bathroom, so I climb the stairs to the third floor. Mr. Lester and Ms. Debbé are standing in Ms. Debbé's office.

"They were here Saturday. This I know," Ms. Debbé is saying. Her French accent is even thicker than usual. "And now . . . look!"

I hear the rustle of tissue paper. I *know* the sound of that tissue paper. I creep around and peek inside. Sure enough, the carved wooden shoe box is on her desk. She's digging through the tissue paper as if the shoes might be lost in it.

Mr. Lester leans over to examine the box.

"You're sure they didn't fall out? Are they in the drawer?"

"Of course they're not in the drawer," Ms. Debbé says. "Miss Camilla Freeman's shoes! Who on earth would do this?"

Mr. Lester paces the floor. I pull back to stay out of sight. "The only people in the building after classes on Saturday were the painters. They worked all weekend, but I'm sure your office was locked."

"Well, it couldn't have been if the shoes are gone," Ms. Debbé says. "Get them on the phone immediately."

"Now, Mom," Mr. Lester says. "How would they know about the shoes? Do you think it could have been one of the students?"

Ms. Debbé draws herself up and glares at him. "My girls, they would never do such a thing. They know how important those shoes are. They know what those shoes mean. It must be those painter men."

My stomach drops to my knees.

Mr. Lester sighs. "Okay. I'll give the head painter a call and ask him."

"You don't *ask* him. You *tell* him. I must have them back," she says. "Whoever took the shoes, they must fire him."

My heart seems to stop beating. (It doesn't really, because I don't keel over dead. Although keeling over dead seems preferable to what I'm about to do.) There are things in life that are really, really bad. And there are things in life that are even worse. Ruining those shoes was really, really bad. But having some painter fired for something I did would be even worse. My feet pull me into the office almost before I realize what is happening.

"Brenda," Mr. Lester says, frowning. "What are you doing up here?"

I inhale deeply. "I took the shoes," I say.

They look at me in disbelief.

"You?" Ms. Debbé looks confused. "But . . .

you are such a good girl. So smart. What would make you do this thing?"

"I wanted to show them to my cousin," I say. "I was going to bring them back."

They're both quiet. I wish they would holler at me or call the police or something. I feel miserable just standing there with their eyes on me.

"Where are the shoes now?" Mr. Lester asks.

"At home," I say. I neglect to mention exactly what condition they're in.

Ms. Debbé's face softens. "Come here, Brenda," she says.

I approach her desk nervously. I wonder if she's going to punch me. Fortunately, punching someone doesn't seem very ladylike, and they're very big on ladylike here at the Nutcracker School. Instead she takes my hand in both of hers. Her hands are warm. I stare down at the rings on her knotted brown fingers.

"I think I know why you do this," she says gently. "Touching those shoes is like touching greatness, is it not? The shoes show us that hard work can overcome even the greatest obstacles. That is why they are such an inspiration to me. I think I can see how also they would be an inspiration to you, an inspiration

88

you would like to have near you just for a lit-tle while."

I keep quiet, even though my insides are lurching around like a ship in a hurricane. Where is this going?

She continues. "Brenda, it was wrong to take the shoes. You know that?"

I nod vigorously.

"But even the best of us succumb to temp-tation sometimes. Yesterday, for example, I had a slice of German chocolate cake. À la mode." She closes her eyes and shakes her head slightly before continuing. "That is why I will do this. If you bring the shoes back on Saturday, I will not mention this to anyone. It will be our secret." She drops my hand. I can still feel the bands of her rings pressing into it.

"But . . ." I begin.

She interrupts. "If you do *not* bring them back on Saturday, I will need to discuss the sit-uation with your mother. Do you understand?"

My legs feel wobbly. I feel the blood rush to my ears. The wall in front of me seems to shimmer. Mom would be furious. She'd ground me for the rest of my life. I would never be able to set foot in the Nutcracker School again. And this is the place where I see all my friends. I imagine sitting at home every Tuesday and Saturday, knowing they're all here together without me.

"I understand," I say.

She nods. "Now. Go warm up for class."

I turn and leave her office. I have exactly four days to figure a way out of this. It seems impossible, but there must be an answer. And somehow, I'm going to find it.

Chapter 10

I walk down the stairs to the waiting room. Terrel, Epatha, Al, and the triplets are clumped together in the back corner. Epatha meets me with a big grin.

"Did you put the shoes back? How did you do it?" she asks.

I look at Terrel. She shakes her head. She hasn't told them.

Al looks at me closely. "Are you okay? You don't look so good."

"Maybe she has beriberi," Jerzey Mae says, alarmed. She takes a step away from me.

I feel Jessica's eyes on me, but I'm so embarrassed I can't look at her. I look at

Jerzey Mae instead. "You have to promise not to scream," I tell her.

She looks at me indignantly. "What makes you think I'd scream? Of course I won't scream."

I look around. Another group of girls is sitting close by. "Shoes the ate dog cousin's my," I say.

Jerzey Mae screams. Everyone in the room turns to stare. JoAnn quickly clamps her hand over her sister's mouth.

"You're kidding!" Al says, after the rest of the kids go back to what they were doing.

"Nope."

"Does Ms. Debbé know the shoes are missing?" whispers Epatha.

"Yep."

"Does she know they've been eaten?" she asks.

"Nope." I slump against the wall. "She says if I bring them back Saturday, she won't tell anyone. And if I don't . . ."

"What?" Epatha interrupts, leaning forward.

"She tells my mom, and then who knows? I wouldn't be surprised if Mom says I can't take ballet anymore."

My friends emit a collective gasp.

Al turns to Terrel. "T., you've gotta think of something!"

Terrel shakes her head. "I've been trying all weekend."

"But you have to!" Al says.

Terrel glares at her. "It's not like I'm Superman and can fly real fast around the world to reverse time or something. Jeez."

We're all quiet for a minute. I look at Jessica. "You were right," I say. "I never should have done this. It was stupid. I don't blame you if you never talk to me again."

She seems to stare right into my soul. She sits up straight. "If we need to get those shoes back by Saturday, we will."

I frown. "Jessica, they are not just *kind* of destroyed. They are *really* destroyed."

"I don't care." Her voice is firm. "We'll find a way. Meeting at our house tomorrow after school. Bring the shoes. All Sugar Plums must attend. Okay?"

We're all surprised to see her take charge. That's usually Terrel's job.

"Okay," we reply.

Jessica's determination gives me a new sense of hope. She's right—there must be a solution. Was Leonardo a quitter? He was not. Maybe there's a chemical in my chemistry set that can make new ballet shoes look old. Scientists can clone a whole sheep from a tiny bit of another sheep. Maybe I can clone a pair of ballet shoes from one of the remaining scraps of Miss Camilla Freeman's.

But I don't have a new pair of shoes to experiment on. And I've only heard of cloning living things, not stuff like shoes. If nonliving things could be cloned, I could clone a dollar over and over till I had enough money to pay Ms. Debbé for her priceless shoes. I can only hope my friends have some better ideas.

After school the next day, Al's mom drops her, Terrel, and me off at the triplets' house. They live in a five-story brownstone in a famous Harlem neighborhood called Strivers' Row. The housekeeper lets us in, since their parents are both at work. My feet sink into the deep carpet in the hall. Their father teaches African studies at a university, so he goes to Africa a lot and brings back interesting stuff, like the cool carved wooden masks staring at us from the wall.

"Hi," Jessica calls from the top of the stairs. We go up. I run my finger along the grooves in the railing, which looks like the kind kids in books are always sliding down.

Each of the triplets has her own room. The rooms, which are connected by doorways, couldn't be more different. JoAnn's is full of skateboards, roller skates, and sports magazines. Her clothes are thrown all over, as if a tidal wave had swept through.

Jerzey Mae's has pink walls, lots of ruffles, and one of those canopy beds with poles holding up a frilly bed roof. The room is as tidy as a hotel room you might see on TV. She's a really good artist, and her paintings and drawings—all exactly the same size—hang on the wall in a neat row.

Jessica's room has a split personality. One side has shelves of books, especially poetry books, and a writing desk, and a little statue of Emily Dickinson.

The other side is where all of Jessica's animals live. There's Herman the iguana, Walt the box turtle, Shakespeare the white rat, and Edgar, the very loud mynah bird. Jessica writes poetry in her room. When she's looking for a rhyming word, she says lists of words out loud. As a result, Edgar recites phrases like "Bat cat fat!" and "Hay may pay!" at the top of his lungs.

We meet in Jerzey's room, since JoAnn's furniture is buried under clothes and Jessica's room is too distracting, what with the scratching noise of iguana claws and Edgar's loud outbursts. Al and Epatha sit on the pink bed. Jessica, Jerzey Mae, Terrel, and I sit on pink chairs. JoAnn sprawls on the pink carpet. Jessica tries to call the meeting to order, but is interrupted by a constant thump, thump-a-bump, thump, thump sound from across the hall.

Al's eyes open wide. "What the heck is that?"

she asks. She's never been to the triplets' house before.

"It's Mason. He's *il loro fratello più giovane*—their little brother," Epatha says. "Mr. Basketball-Star-in-Training."

"He practices dribbling all day long. ALL day," JoAnn says with a sigh. She goes across the hall and pounds on his door. "Mason! Knock it off!"

Mason doesn't knock it off.

Jessica raises her voice and continues.

"We all know why we're here. We have to find a way to get Miss Camilla Freeman's shoes back. One idea I had is to repair them. Jerzey is exceptionally good at crafts."

Jerzey smiles at her and looks a little embarrassed.

Jessica turns to me. "Did you bring the shoes?"

I slowly unzip my backpack and pull out the misshapen blobs of fabric and leather.

The ribbons, full of holes, dangle down to the floor. They swing halfheartedly for a second, then stop as though they've given up.

Everyone gasps. Epatha whistles a long, low whistle.

"I don't care how good Jerzey is," Epatha says. "She's not good enough to fix that mess."

Jessica looks a little shaken. "All right," she says, composing herself. "We will not repair the shoes. So, we need to brainstorm."

"We need to *what*?" asks Terrel.

Jessica pulls up a big pad of paper. "Something I learned in my creative writing class last summer. It's what you do when you think of all the ideas you possibly can, even if they're silly. No one's allowed to laugh. You just yell things out. I'll write them down; then we can see if any of them might work." She uncaps a felt-tipped marker. "Okay . . . go!"

"*Car star tar!*" we hear from the next room.

"Quiet, Edgar!" Jessica calls out. "Humans only."

"Buy another pair of shoes," JoAnn says.

"Where are we gonna buy fifty-year-old shoes?" Epatha asks.

"You can buy anything on the Internet," JoAnn replies. "A boy in my class bought fossilized dinosaur poop on the Internet."

"That is revolting," Jerzey Mae says.

Jessica whistles for attention. "Just shout out ideas. Any ideas. Stupid ideas. Don't worry about how we'll do them."

At first I have trouble with this. I do not like to look stupid, and I do not like stupid ideas on principle. But my friends jump right in. Soon we're all shouting out ideas, which get sillier and sillier.

"Hypnotize Ms. Debbé so she forgets she ever had the shoes," yells Al.

"Get a matter duplicator from an alien spaceship to make a new pair," says Terrel.

100

"Find Miss Camilla Freeman and ask her for another pair of shoes!" I holler.

Jessica stops cold and stares at me.

"What?" I ask. I feel my cheeks get hot. "You said they could be stupid ideas."

Jessica tears out of the room like her shoes are on fire. We hear soft thumps as she runs down the carpeted stairs.

"Wow," Epatha says. "Your idea must have been even stupider than she expected."

In a minute we hear Jessica thumping back up the steps. She bursts back into the room carrying a newspaper.

"Jessica, this is not really the time to catch up on current events," Jerzey Mae says.

"Shhh," Jessica says, pulling out a section of the paper and flipping through it, fingers flying.

"Aha!" she cries. She points to the corner of the page.

JoAnn peers over her shoulder. "The

Haunted Book Shoppe," JoAnn reads. "You think they have a book about how to bring ballet shoes back from the dead?"

"Not that one—*this* one." Jessica points to another advertisement. "Crowe & Company Book Shop. See what's happening there?"

Jerzey Mae squints at the small print. "So, they have authors coming to sign their books. Lots of bookstores do that. Dad had a book signing when his book came out."

Jessica shakes the paper with impatience. "Look who's coming on September twenty-ninth. This Friday."

We all lean over the paper to see.

"Miss Camilla Freeman!" we shout together.

"How the heck did you find that?" JoAnn looks at Jessica with grudging admiration.

Jessica tosses the paper aside. "I was looking for poetry readings, because Mom promised she'd take me to one this week if I could find one that wasn't too far away. I

noticed Miss Camilla Freeman's name, but I
didn't put things together till just now."

"Put what together?" I ask. It would be
cool to see Miss Camilla Freeman and all, but
I don't see how . . .

I stare at Jessica. "You don't mean . . ."

She gives me a firm look. "Yes. We are
going to go see Miss Camilla Freeman and ask
her if she'll give us a pair of her toeshoes."

Chapter 11

The room falls silent.

"How?" Jerzey Mae finally asks.

We all look at Terrel. She's scrunching up her eyes and poking at her teeth with her tongue, which is a good sign. She points at me. "*You're* gonna have to do the asking," she says. "But I can get you to the bookstore."

"Get *us* to the bookstore," Jessica corrects her. She drapes her arm around my back. "I'm going, too. For moral support."

Epatha comes over and stands behind us, her hands on her hips. "Add me to that list, T."

Terrel looks around the room. "We're all going?"

JoAnn, Jerzey Mae, and Al nod. Al winks at

me. I'm so relieved that my eyes start tingling. I blink hard.

Terrel nods. "That makes it a little easier. We need a grown-up to take us, but not a nosy grown-up. Epatha, would Amarah do it?"

Amarah is Epatha's biggest sister. She's not a real grown-up, because she's still in college, but she's close enough.

Epatha nods. "*Certo*. Of course. I saw her sneak out to meet her boyfriend last night, but I didn't tell Papa. She owes me one."

JoAnn picks the newspaper up off the floor. "Where is this place, anyway? Is it in Harlem?" She finds the advertisement again. "It's in midtown. We'll have to take the sub- way."

"What time is Miss Camilla Freeman going to be at the bookstore?" Terrel asks.

JoAnn looks. "From four p.m. to six p.m."

"We should get there at the beginning," Terrel says.

Jerzey Mae shakes her head. "When Daddy did his reading, they hid him somewhere before it started, so everyone would clap when he came out."

"Okay, so I guess we'll have to catch her right at the end," says Terrel. "Let's meet at the subway at 125th Street at five on Friday. That should get us there in plenty of time."

I can tell everyone's excited. I am too. We have a plan. All my friends are behind me. Things don't seem quite so hopeless anymore.

Jessica smiles at me. "It will be an adventure."

"Miss Camilla *who*?" my mom asks. She's letting out the hem on one of my pairs of pants. According to her, I'm growing like a weed, which I think is rather inelegant. I would prefer to grow like an interesting strain of bacteria.

"Miss Camilla Freeman," I say patiently.

"The first black prima ballerina with the Ballet Company of New York. She's Ms. Debbé's idol."

Mom snips another thread. "Is this for your ballet class?" she asks.

Well, if this plan doesn't work, Mom will find out and ground me till I'm thirty, which would essentially end my ballet career. "Yes," I say, hopping up and down on one foot. But I keep thinking, what if she says no?

She puts the pants aside and sighs. "Then I suppose you can go. But I think you should take Tiffany, too. You know she likes ballet, and she's probably feeling left out just sitting around while you're at school."

The last thing I need is one more thing to worry about on this crazy trip. "I'm afraid that would not be polite," I say. "Amarah already has to watch all seven of us. If we add one more, she might have a conniption fit." I am not sure what a conniption fit is—it's not in any of my disease books—but Epatha's mom worried about Epatha's grandma's having one when Epatha got her ears pierced.

Mom looks surprised. "That's very considerate of you, Brenda. You're probably right."

Shocked, I turn and go to my room. I guess good manners do have a purpose after all.

On Friday Mom drops me off at the subway entrance, where Epatha and Amarah are waiting.

"You have your subway card?" Mom asks.

I reach into my pocket and pull out my card to show her.

"And money for a pay phone if you need to call me?" she says.

"Yes," I say. As if there's a pay phone anywhere in New York that actually works.

"And . . ."

"Mom!" I interrupt. "I'm not going away to college. We're just going downtown."

"Okay, okay," she says. "You have a good time." I catch her peeking over her shoulder at us as she walks back up the street.

Epatha grabs Amarah's wrist and turns it around so she can peer at her watch. "Where *is* everybody?" she asks.

Just as she says that, the triplets and Al walk up behind her, along with Al's mom. Well, Jerzey and Jessica walk; JoAnn zooms up on her skateboard, which she then flips neatly into the air. Al and her mom have a conversation that is almost identical to the one I just had with my mom.

At 5:15, Terrel races up with her brother Cheng. "Sorry," she pants. "*Someone* had to watch the end of his TV show." She whacks Cheng on the arm. He rolls his eyes, then lopes off down the street without a word.

"Let's get this show on the road," Amarah says, herding us all to the entrance of the subway station.

We walk down the stairs and head for the turnstiles. The station is teeming with people. "You all just *had* to go downtown during rush hour, didn't you?" Amarah asks, sighing heavily.

"Miss Camilla Freeman did not contact us before she scheduled her signing," Epatha says.

We swipe our MetroCards into the turnstile and pass through, then walk down another set of stairs. "Keep together," Amarah says.

We bunch together on the crowded platform, surrounded by old people, young people, people in jeans, people in suits, and people wearing too much stinky cologne. A train barrels into the station and we push inside. There aren't many places to sit, so Jessica, JoAnn, and I find seats while the others look around for poles to grab.

The train starts, and we scramble to keep

our balance. As it pulls into various stations, people shove to get off and shove to get on. "We're getting off at Fifty-ninth Street!" Amarah hollers over the train's rumbling and clanking. "So, pay attention."

The wristwatch of the woman in front of me reads 5:25. "Are we going to get there in time?" I whisper to Epatha.

"No problemo," she says. "It should only take ten or fifteen minutes."

Just as she says this, the train screeches to a halt. The lights flicker, then go off. Jerzey's fingers dig into my arm.

"Ow!" I holler.

"Sorry," she says. Her voice is five times higher than normal.

The train gets so quiet I can hear Jerzey's fast breathing. I wonder if she's going to hyperventilate. When people do that you're supposed to give them a paper bag to breathe into. I don't have a paper bag. I wonder if a backpack would work.

A guy on the other side of the train yells, *"Woo-ooo-OOO-ooo-ooo!"* like a deranged ghost. Some people snicker. Jerzey Mae's fingers clutch my arm even harder.

"Oh, man," Epatha says.

"What's happening?" I ask.

"Who knows?" says Amarah.

The lights flicker again, then come back on. But the train stays stuck. A woman's voice crackles over the announcement system.

"We have a red signal. We should be moving momentarily. Thank you for your patience."

My stomach twists up in knots. "What time is it now?" I ask Epatha's sister. She shows me her watch. We only have twenty-five minutes before Miss Camilla Freeman leaves the bookstore.

Al looks at me. "Are we going to make it?" she asks.

"How far from the subway to the store?" Terrel asks Amarah.

"Just a five-minute walk," Amarah says. "No sweat." She glances at her watch again.

Time seems to stretch into hours. I wish someone would say something. "I don't suppose you have a Plan B?" I whisper to Terrel.

"Yeah," she says. "Friendly aliens are going to beam us up to their ship, then down to the bookstore." I don't ask her any more questions.

Finally, after what feels like days, the train shudders, starts rolling slowly, then picks up speed and pulls into the Ninety-sixth Street station.

I start breathing again. "How many more stops?" I ask.

"Four," says Amarah.

"Four?" My foot flaps up and down as if it's trying to take off. *Hurry, hurry, hurry*, I chant to myself.

When the doors slide open at Fifty-ninth Street, we burst out like popcorn exploding from a popper. The clock on the wall reads 5:57. The escalator's clogged with people, so we tear up the stairs.

"Where's the store?" I pant as we reach the top.

"Two blocks that way," Amarah says.

"We're not going to make it!" Jerzey squeals.

JoAnn jumps onto her skateboard. "I'll go

114

ahead and try to keep Miss Freeman from leaving," she says. She looks at Amarah.

Amarah hesitates. She studies the street, then nods. "We'll be right behind you," she says.

JoAnn zooms toward the store, weaving in and out of the crowds on the sidewalk. We follow her like a pack of wolves—all except Al, who gapes up at the huge towers of the Time Warner Center (she hasn't lived in New York very long); Jessica has to drag her along. Amarah strains to keep JoAnn in sight as our sneakers pound the sidewalk. Up ahead we see JoAnn leap off her board and dash inside the store.

We arrive at the bookstore panting and wheezing. Just as Epatha reaches for the door handle, JoAnn comes out, shoulders slumped.

"We missed her," she says. "They said she just left."

We stand there in silence.

"Well, that's it, then," I finally say. "I'm toast."

Jessica puts her arm around my shoulders. Al looks miserable. A group of people push past us to go inside.

"Let's get out of the way." Amarah pulls us around to the side of the store, where we huddle by an unmarked green door. Next to us is a window displaying Miss Camilla Freeman's book, *Dance Through the Storms*. An elderly woman smiles from the cover. APPEARING HERE TODAY, says a sign in the window.

"Whole lot of good it did us," Terrel mutters.

The door beside us opens and two people come out. The man is tall and wears a uniform. The woman is old, tiny, and birdlike.

"Excuse us, girls," the woman says. She and the man walk past us and over to a big black car parked beside the store. The man bends over to open the door for her.

Terrel's eyes open wide as she looks from the book display in the store window to the woman's face. "That's her!" she hisses. "That's Miss Camilla Freeman!"

I freeze. But JoAnn doesn't. "Miss Freeman!" she yells. "Miss Freeman! We need to talk to you!"

JoAnn takes my hand and drags me over to the car. The other girls follow.

Miss Camilla Freeman looks at me expectantly. "Yes?" she says.

"Um . . ." My mouth feels like it's full of wet cement. "I . . . well, I . . ."

"We go to the Nutcracker School," Epatha interrupts. "And Ms. Debbé has a pair of your old toeshoes . . ."

". . . And Brenda here borrowed them to show her cousin Tiffany," says Terrel.

". . . But a dog ate them," says Jerzey Mae.

". . . And Ms. Debbé doesn't know," says JoAnn.

". . . And if we don't get the shoes back, Brenda might not be able to take ballet anymore," says Al.

". . . So we were wondering if you could give us another pair of autographed toeshoes," Jessica says.

Miss Camilla Freeman's dark eyes settle on mine. "Is this true?" she asks.

I nod. I feel horrible. How could I have ever thought this would be easier than just coming clean and telling Ms. Debbé what I'd done? And why, *why*, did I have to take the shoes?

Miss Camilla Freeman looks up past my head. I wonder what she's staring at until I hear a familiar voice say, "Very interesting."

I turn around. Ms. Debbé is standing behind us, holding a stack of Miss Camilla Freeman's books in her arms.

Chapter 12

Ms. Debbé does not look happy. No one says a word.

Miss Camilla Freeman looks from Ms. Debbé to me and back again. "I think," she finally says, "that matters like this are best settled over a civilized cup of tea. Don't you agree, Miss . . . ?" She turns to Amarah.

"Amarah," she says.

"And you, Adrienne?" she asks Ms. Debbé.

Without waiting for an answer, Miss Camilla Freeman leads us back to the bookstore. The man in the uniform races ahead to open the door for her. She sweeps in, and we all follow. Ms. Debbé is behind me. I feel her eyes burning into me like laser beams.

We go up the escalators to the bookstore café. "Tea and cakes for everyone, George," she tells the man. He walks to the counter as we sit down at a big, round table. We sit in silence until George brings over a big pot of tea and plates of little cakes and sandwiches.

Miss Camilla Freeman pours out tea for us. I've never had real tea before. I take a sip.

"You might like it better with milk and sugar," Miss Camilla Freeman says. Jerzey Mae is drinking elegantly, as though she has tea with a ballet star every day. JoAnn looks as if she's afraid to pick up the cup for fear of dropping it.

"Now," Miss Camilla Freeman says, "tell me these things once again. Slowly this time."

I take a deep breath. This time I tell her the whole story myself, because, after all, it's all my fault. I tell her about how I was jealous of Tiffany. I tell her how I only meant to borrow the shoes. I tell her about Pookiepie.

Miss Camilla Freeman looks around at everyone. "Did all of you take shoes, too? Why are you here?"

"No," says Epatha. "We're here because we're *sus amigas*, her friends."

The other Sugar Plum Sisters nod.

"And did you meet in Ms. Debbé's ballet class?" she asks.

"Yes," I say.

Miss Camilla Freeman smiles at Ms. Debbé. "You see what your class has done? These girls didn't know each other before, and now they're friends." She looks around at us. "Very good friends, it seems. Ballet is important. But friendships are even more important."

"You're not going to make Brenda leave our class, are you, Ms. Debbé?" Jessica bursts out.

Ms. Debbé's face hardens. "Those shoes were very special to me," she says.

Miss Camilla Freeman nods. "Well. There are two things I want you to think about before you decide," she says to Ms. Debbé. "One is this: do you know how many pairs of toeshoes I went through each week when I danced? Eight! And I could not bear to throw any away. So, I will gladly give you another pair. You can even choose which ballet."

"Oh . . ." Ms. Debbé says. "Even *Swan Lake*?"

"Even *Swan Lake*," Miss Camilla Freeman says.

Ms. Debbé looks off into the distance. I think I might be off the hook. But then she shakes her head. "Still. I cannot allow a student to do something like this and go unpunished."

"Then there is one more thing for you to think about," Miss Camilla Freeman says. "I remember many years ago, when I was living in the dormitory of the Ballet Company of

New York. Some of the young girls who were studying dance at our academy lived there, too. One day I found that one of them—a very talented girl who was usually a model of good behavior—had taken a tutu from the costume department, because she wanted so badly to try it on. The tutu ripped. The girl was in a panic when she told me. We stayed up late into the night fixing the tutu so we could return it before its absence was discovered."

We all exchange puzzled looks. What did that have to do with anything?

Ms. Debbé, looks extremely uncomfortable for some reason. She shifts in her chair and coughs several times. Miss Camilla Freeman wears a placid expression.

Ms. Debbé quickly takes a sip of tea. She pats her lips with a napkin, then clears her throat. "I think," she says, "that under the circumstances, we can perhaps forget about this shoe incident."

Miss Camilla Freeman claps her hands together. "Very good!" she says. "Now. Let us all enjoy our lovely cakes."

As we eat, Miss Camilla Freeman regales us with stories about dancing with the Ballet Company of New York. She tells us what it was like to be a black dancer back then, when almost all ballet dancers were white.

"Ms. Debbé says your toeshoes represent

potential," Jessica says. "She tells us that all the time."

JoAnn adds, "And she tells us if we want to do something, like be a famous skateboarder, we should stick to it and not give up."

"I do not remember *specifically* mentioning skateboarding," Ms. Debbé says, looking at JoAnn out of the corner of her eye.

Miss Camilla Freeman tilts her head and

smiles. "You teach your students very well, Adrienne," she says to Ms. Debbé. "I'm proud of you."

A strange expression crosses Ms. Debbé's face, and her eyes get a little watery. But a second later she seems like herself again, strong and composed. "Girls, we must let Miss Camilla Freeman get home. She has had a busy day signing books."

Miss Camilla Freeman stands up. "Yes. But I will walk, because I need some exercise after sitting all day. Adrienne, if you will walk with me, perhaps George will be so kind as to take these young ladies home?"

George tips his hat.

"In that big old limousine?" Epatha asks, awestruck.

George nods.

"Wow!" Epatha says.

We pile into the plush backseat and ride home to Harlem in style, gliding through traffic. We giggle. We whoop. We pretend to drink champagne from the glasses in the back. George opens the top of the limo and we take turns sticking our heads out and hollering at people.

"They probably think we're important," Al says as we wave at a family sitting out on their front steps.

"We *are* important," Epatha says. "We are the Sugar Plum Sisters, and we have just completed a successful mission. We have gotten our sister Brenda off the hook, and we have gotten Ms. Debbé an even better pair of toeshoes. Miss Camilla Freeman is not the only one who has had a busy day."

Epatha's right—everything really did work out okay. I smile and sink back into the soft cushions. As we weave through traffic, the weight that's been pressing down on me finally lifts.

Chapter 13

Mom and Tiffany happen to be coming home from the grocery store when the limo pulls up in front of my apartment building. Tiffany's eyes look as if they might pop out of her head. So, unfortunately, do Mom's.

"What on earth . . ." Mom says, as George opens the door and I step out.

"I'll . . . uh, I'll tell you inside," I say. I

thank George and wave as the limousine pulls away from the curb.

If the ballet slippers didn't impress Tiffany enough, this certainly does. I realize that she finally thinks I'm important. And just as I realize this, I also realize I don't care what she thinks anymore. Trying to impress Tiffany got me into the worst mess I've ever been in in my whole life. It didn't matter to Miss Camilla Freeman if I had fancy clothes, or a computer, or an iPod. Like she said, friends are what's important. And I've got the best friends in the world.

We all sit at the kitchen table. I tell Mom everything that happened. I could have made something up, but I'm done with all that.

"Well," she says. "Well . . ."

I wait for her to tell me I'm being punished, but she changes the subject.

"Tiffany's dad called while you were gone," she says. "He and Thelma got back early, so Tiffany's leaving tomorrow. Why don't you two go and get things packed up? Brenda, we can discuss this more later."

Tiffany stands up, then looks at Mom. "Please don't tell my mom that Pookiepie ate the shoes, okay?"

Mom smiles. "She never did like animals much, did she? When we were kids, she pretended she was allergic to my cat Freddie because Freddie clawed up her favorite blanket. Nope, your secret's safe with me." She stands up and puts her arm around Tiffany's shoulders.

"Besides, it wasn't Pookiepie's fault—*someone* shouldn't have taken the shoes in the first place." Mom looks at me over the top of her glasses.

"Well, we'd better help you pack up," I say quickly, pulling Tiffany out of the kitchen.

As soon as we get to my room, Tiffany turns to me.

"Why did you tell me you had the toeshoes when you didn't?" she asks.

"I was jealous of you," I say. "You're always talking about all the stuff you have. I wanted to have something that would make you jealous."

Tiffany looks at me. She's quiet for a minute. Then she says, "You already do."

I look at her as if she's crazy. "What do I have that you could possibly want? You have everything."

She shakes her head. "My mom's gone all the time. She and dad buy me things, but they're never around. You joke around with your mom and hug her and stuff. I wish we were friends like you guys are."

I try to wrap my head around this new idea. I thought Tiffany had the perfect life, and all the time she was jealous of *me*. Life is pretty weird sometimes.

"Maybe you can hang out with us more," I

say. "Want to come over for alphabet pasta on Sunday?"

Tiffany smiles, not an I'm-better-than-you smile, but a real one. "Yeah," she says. "Maybe you can tell me more about that Leonardo guy."

We hear a skittering sound and a snort from under the bed. I lift up the bed-skirt. Pookiepie's paws are wrapped around my slippers, which now have a decorative pattern of holes chewed through the soles.

"Um, Tiffany? On Sunday . . ."

She reaches under the bed and scoops him out. "On Sunday, Pookiepie will stay home."

Chapter 14

Saturday, after Tiffany leaves, I write a letter of apology to Ms. Debbé. Mom says this is a good start, but I suspect there is at least a month of additional chores in my future as well. I know that what I did was really wrong, and really stupid, and I will never, ever, do anything that idiotic again.

But even though it was wrong and stupid, I can't help seeing the good things that have come out of it. I explain to Mom that if I hadn't taken the shoes, Ms. Debbé would still have her old Miss Camilla Freeman shoes, not the extraspecial *Swan Lake* ones; plus, all my friends would never have gotten to have tea with a world-famous ballerina. Still, Mom thinks I should be punished. As I said, she does not have a very logical mind.

When I get to the Nutcracker School, I put the letter in Ms. Debbé's mail slot. Then I go into the waiting room. All the Sugar Plum Sisters are there by our usual bench.

"Hey," I say, plunking down between JoAnn and Jerzey Mae.

"Glad you're here," JoAnn grins.

Tiara Girl walks by. "Guess where we were last night?" Epatha calls to her. "Having tea with Miss Camilla Freeman. What do you think about that?"

Tiara Girl tosses her hair. "I am *so* sure."

"Ask Ms. Debbé, if you don't believe us," Epatha says with a smirk.

Tiara Girl looks confused, like this can't possibly be happening. "I will," she says.

"Good," says Epatha. We all exchange grins.

Just then, Ms. Debbé appears in the doorway. She's carrying the carved wooden shoe box.

"The *Swan Lake* shoes!" Al says.

JoAnn rolls her eyes. "Great. Now we have to hear the Shoe Talk *twice* in one session." She shoves me.

Ms. Debbé taps her walking stick for attention. Then she says the words I was afraid I'd never hear again.

"The class, it begins."

Jessica wraps her arm around me, and we start to climb the stairs.

I stop and turn to her. "Promise me something."

"What?" she asks, her eyes big.

"Shoes those steal me let *ever* never," I say.

Jessica grins, and we continue up the stairs, our friends right behind us.

Terms Ballet
to Guide Brenda's
(Translated from backward writing by Al)

châiné turns—fast turns that move in one direction. To do these, you need a functional **vestibular system**.

Leonardo da Vinci—the brilliant Italian scientist, mathematician, inventor, and painter who lived from 1452 to 1519. I know this is not exactly related to ballet, but everyone should know about him.

Mona Lisa—Leonardo's most famous painting. Again, not exactly ballet-related, but see above.

pirouette—a turn done on one leg. Also requires a **vestibular system**.

plié—knee-bend. Requires the use of many of your leg muscles, including the adductor magnus and the vastus lateralis.

podiatrist—foot doctor. I am *not* planning to be one of these when I grow up. Feet are very interesting, but I don't want to stare at them (or smell them) all day long.

pointe, dancing on—dancing on the tips of your toes, which were not designed to be danced on like that. May have been invented to keep **podiatrists** in business.

pointe shoes, or **toeshoes**—shoes with boxy toes you wear when dancing on pointe. If your teacher keeps some in a box in her desk, do NOT borrow them.

Especially if your cousin's shoe-chewing dog is visiting.

Swan Lake—famous ballet about a princess who got turned into a swan. This is illogical, not to mention physiologically impossible.

vestibular system—part of the inner ear that helps you keep your balance. Extremely important in ballet. Before Al learned to turn correctly last summer, I wondered if hers was missing. (Very funny, Brenda—Al)